THE GIRLS THEY STOLE

THE AUCTION TRILOGY

J.H. LEIGH

J.H. LEIGH

CONTENTS

COPYRIGHT

THE GIRLS THEY STOLE

By J.H Leigh

Cover design by Richer Designs

The following **NOVEL** is approximately 51,000 words and previously published under the title *No One To Notice* by Angel James.

A NOTE FROM JH

Dear Reader,

Sometimes stories come to you in a flash of stunning violence and epic clarity. The first draft of this story poured from my fingers in nearly one sitting. I've come to learn when creative lightning strikes, you follow where it leads.

I am so grateful for the vision needed to create this series. It's dark, deep, emotional and timely. Trauma affects everyone differently but for every victim who felt cowed and defeated, I hope this series finds you healed and whole by the spirit of three young girls who refused to be beaten.

All my love,

J.H. Leigh

BACK COVER BLURB

The deal seems easy. Follow the rules. Keep your mouth shut. The payoff? Enough money to change your life forever.

But is it too good to be true?

Nicole, Dylan, Jilly and Tana need to take the deal. All for different, equally desperate reasons. But the deal comes at a price. Once they step into Madame Moirai's depraved world it's too late. All four come face to face with the darkest depths of humanity lurking beneath the glitter of extreme wealth and elite privilege. Innocent, vulnerable girls are drugged and dragged to the auction block, their humanity stripped, and sold to the highest bidder.

The crowd, billionaires, politicians, and the rich and famous compete to win the choicest girls.

No one cares about their pain. No one protests the debauchery.

Not even when one of the girls ends up dead.

Under lock and key by guards, bound by soul-searing trauma, the girls must work together if they're going to survive.

There is no in-between — and the clock is ticking.

Madame Moirai doesn't tolerate loose ends...or girls who speak when they should remain silent.

PROLOGUE

Shine on friend. Goodnight
Why, then, the darkening of the light?
— Johnette Lin Napolitano

We all die alone.

But she died crying, begging, bleeding. *Broken.*

Who made up the rule that eighteen was more mature than seventeen? A 24-hour space in time didn't change the fact that she signed away her life without realizing it would be her end.

She'd wanted what we all wanted — *hope.*

But the wicked feasted on the desperate, luring with the promise of something they'd never give.

And innocence remained the most stolen currency in a world that'd lost its soul.

We all signed on for the same deal.

We had no idea how it would ruin us.

They had no idea how I would ruin them.

THIS IS OUR STORY.

1

I, Nicole Esther West, give Madame Moirai the right to act as my agent at The Auction for the sum of 40 percent of any and all transactions conducted at said auction.

The sharp black words blurred on the page as my eyes glazed over and a voice whispered, _don't do it_, but I wasn't backing out — not a chance. I needed this as desperately as I needed air to breathe.

I shifted against the itch of shame that scratched at my conscience. No one knew my life, they didn't get an opinion about what I do.

My nerves were strung tight and my stomach hurt. This wasn't the kind of anxiety you get before a mid-term you didn't study for — that'd be easy — this was the jitters that happened when you're about to make the biggest decision of your life.

Most girls never had to make a choice like this. Girls from nice, stable families were never asked.

I gripped the pen more tightly as I reread the fine print but the words were blurring and my palms were clammy.

My one and only chance to get out, to create a life that wasn't contaminated by the woman who'd given birth to me but otherwise failed as a mother. Carla West was like a herpes infection, stuck to me for life, unless I could scrape up enough money for the miracle vaccine.

That's what this document was giving me — a first-class ticket to the rest of my life.

I wanted to leave this ratchet piece of urban nothing and forget the first seventeen years of my life. Erase it from my memory. Maybe even change my name. I wanted to go to college with a clean slate.

Dreams were dangerous things. Hope, even more so. Daring to reach for something just beyond your fingertips wasn't something most girls like me ever tried.

I was smart but my grades told a different story. Hard to study when your mom was screaming in the other room, breaking shit, or fighting with the grabby slob of the moment. Also hard to keep up with the curriculum when your mom liked to play, "Where's Nicole's math book?" because she hated her daughter rising above her in any way.

I couldn't pay the fine for lost books. Couldn't get another book unless I paid the fine. *You get where I'm going?* It was a vicious cycle designed to drag you down but I tried my damnedest to keep my head above water. Poverty was an endless whirlpool sucking the life out of everything it touched. Counselors liked to preach at me, "Nicole, you're so smart but you need to apply yourself..." and I wanted to yell back, "Bitch, you don't know what I have to deal with so fuck off with your useless advice."

I didn't say that, though. I couldn't get kicked out of school. School was the only sanctuary I had. It was the only place I was free of Carla. So, I swallowed my rage and promised to try harder, appeasing the fat, middle-aged counselor whose fading blonde hair looked as tired as her dehydrated skin.

Until Madame Moirai dangled her offer in front of my face. Suddenly, I had options. The way I saw it, I'd be a fool not to grab that offer and run with it, even if the thought made my skin crawl.

As long as I didn't chicken out — and trust me, there were plenty of valid reasons to back the fuck out — I'd come out the other side free from my toxic mother.

I scribbled my name as fast as I could, the scratch of the pen echoing in my head, loud and incriminating.

If anyone found out, I'd never live down the shame. I would take this dirty secret to my grave. Opportunity didn't always show up looking like a fairy godmother. Sometimes it showed up with gnarled fingers, hungry eyes and a stench of wickedness that would cling to your nostrils until you died.

But desperation bred recklessness, and I was plenty desperate.

What am I doing? I returned the pen with shaking fingers to the emissary. *Whatever is necessary.*

"This document is binding," he reminded me with cold, dead eyes. "Breaching the contract will reap *unfortunate* consequences."

He didn't need to translate. I could figure out what he meant. I was jumping into the deep end of the pool without assurances that I wouldn't land on cement. Nobody was coming to save me. Felt pretty familiar. Like always, I'd save myself.

The nondisclosure clause stood out, almost screaming at me from the document. No running to the cops crying foul.

Like I wanted to shout to the world that I'd sold my V card to a complete stranger. *Yeah, gonna put that tidbit on my Christmas cards. Good icebreaker at parties.*

"I'm sure you're a good girl who honors her commitments, yes?" The man smiled, tucking the neatly folded document into his inside breast pocket of his crisp suit. At my short nod, he continued, "A car will come for you when the time is right. In the meantime, you will have time to complete your bloodwork as well as complete your menstrual cycle."

I swallowed, trying to hold on to my bravery with slippery fingers. I wasn't a good girl if I was doing this. No one would ever consider me a good girl if they knew. Not that I cared what others thought. I'd spent my life fighting against the judgment of others for circumstances out of my control.

This time, I was in control.

"Excellent. We'll be in touch." He gestured for me to leave the confines of the big, black Towncar like I was stinking up the fine Italian leather. I scooted out, and the car left me behind as if it'd never been there. I stood, forlorn and awkward in the empty parking lot of the long-ago bankrupt shopping mall, waiting for my Uber, my body beginning to shake in the darkening light of dusk.

I'd just consented to selling my virginity to the highest bidder. My mouth began to water as my stomach threatened to spill the remnants of my lunch onto the cracked pavement. *Get it down, don't throw up.* This was just another moment I had to get through in my life. One and done. Life forever changed. Seemed a fair trade.

If I'd lived a normal life, I wouldn't approve either, but that wasn't the hand dealt me. Either you adjust and move on or silently agree to be a victim for the rest of your life. *Fuck that shit. I'm no victim.* My Gran used to tell me, some people were born with a stubborn streak stronger than anything meant to break them down. She said I was born with the hard-headed determination of a donkey that dreamed of being a thoroughbred some day. By her thinking, that'd been a compliment.

I missed that chain-smoking locomotive of a woman. Maybe if she hadn't died when I was six, life would've turned out different but playing the 'What If?' game was too hard on the heart to play for long.

Madame Moirai, a woman whose identity no one

knew, contacted me a few weeks ago via her emissary, the thin, impeccably dressed man who'd left me stranded. As if selling yourself wasn't degrading enough, being tossed out like trash for someone else to deal with was the cherry on top.

The transaction itself had been dry and to the point. If the emissary had any personal feelings about the subject, he buried it so deep not even an eyelid twitch gave him away.

The even moderate tone of his voice still echoed in my head, reminding me that there was no going back.

"All buyers are thoroughly vetted with extensive background checks. Your safety — overall — is of the highest importance..."

Selling sex of any kind was still illegal in most states, including liberal-leaning New York. I could go to jail for agreeing to this arrangement.

I was trying to escape a prison, not get locked up in one with different walls.

"However, you may leave the experience with bruises. Some of our patrons, in their exuberance, leave marks. Nothing permanent, I assure you."

The potential for pain loomed in my immediate future. Pain didn't scare me. I'd been beaten enough times in my life to know how to survive a punch. I liked to know what to prepare for. The trick was to be someone else, be somewhere else in your head. Anywhere but in the leaky basement, the smell of mildew and sadness following every swing while your mother worked out her demons on your young skin. Yeah, I had skills for handling pain. I was probably a walking endorsement for future therapy but that was a problem for another day.

"Do you have questions?"

Questions. So many. None mattered. The current would take the boat wherever it wished. I was just along for the ride.

And the payday.

"Do not hope for more than one night with your patron. Attachments are forbidden and will be harshly discouraged. Do you understand?"

Why would anyone want to spend more than one night with these perverts? In my version of a fairytale romance, Prince Charming wasn't a sex-trafficking asshole with a thing for young girls but hey, each to his own, right?

It would be one night of my life. I could handle this.

When you grow up with a shitty parent, you mature real quick. I wasn't squeamish about sex. I wasn't a virgin because I'd been afraid of a dick.

After all the pieces of shit my mom dragged home, I'd seen too much to seek out that drama. Between the thugs who used my mom as a punching bag to the fuckers who leered at me through half-slitted eyes, I had enough to remind me that men were trouble. I also didn't want to deal with unwanted pregnancy or the threat of STDs, because condoms left a margin of error. I wasn't about to take any chances.

Abstinence had seemed easier.

To avoid a dick all this time only to accept the sordid offer from Madame Moirai was irony at its best.

Calm the feminine rage on my behalf. I knew I was more than just a walking vagina but let's be real; we lived in a patriarchal society and women were bought and sold all the time.

Sometimes it's prettied up and called marriage other times...it's just a business transaction.

This kind of thing has been happening since the dawn of time, which was why I was, sort of, prag-matic about it.

How much money was on the table?

According to Mr. Personality, it varied. Depended on the auction crowd. Depended on the product.

But as he so eloquently and bluntly put it, "Any sum of money would be more than you would get from the fumbling attentions of a boy your age, wouldn't you say?"

Hard to argue that point.

A text from a burner phone detailed my instructions. So many rules.

Fresh pineapple daily

No dairy

No refined sugar

No sexual relations of any sort

And the list went on and on.

Any deviation or failure to adhere to the list would be considered a breach of contract. I didn't want to think about what happened to girls who broke the rules. Even though everything to this point had been black and white and to the point, there'd been an inherent air of danger drifting around the confines of the car like a fine layer of smoke that you couldn't exactly see but you could smell.

Madame Moirai wasn't fucking around. This wasn't a game. The stakes were high and the threat real if I failed to uphold my end of the bargain. I wanted to reassure the man I wouldn't bail but my lips had gone numb.

I was making the worst mistake of my life or I was buying my ticket to freedom.

Time would tell.

In the meantime...I had to act like nothing had changed — which meant dealing with my fucking mother.

2

I made it home just in time for my mother to wake up from her vodka stupor, which was always a treat. Today must've been her day off. *Lucky me.*

"What are you doing, whore?" she slurred and for a minute I froze. Did she know? How could she? Oh, wait, calling me a whore was her go-to when she couldn't pull my name from her alcohol-soaked brain. I ignored her and kept moving. Maybe I'd make it to my room before she could stop me.

"I've been calling you for hours. Where the fuck you been?" *Ahh, fake parental concern. How touching.* "I'm almost out of smokes. You gotta make a run for me." And, there's the real reason she was hot to get me on the phone.

I muttered a quick lie, "My phone died," and

pushed open my door. I didn't bother shutting it behind me. The thin particleboard was no match for my mother when she was dead set on getting in and I didn't want to replace another door when she busted it down. "I have homework," I told her, bouncing on my bed and grabbing my backpack.

"Homework. Fuck that. Like you're going anywhere." Her frizzy auburn hair stood on end like she'd stuck her tongue in an electrical outlet. Pictures hidden in a drawer told me Carla had once been beautiful but now, she was a scary caricature of a woman teetering on the edge of her own humanity. Broken dreams and the constant bitterness of disillusionment had a way of chipping away at a person's soul. At this point, my mother was nothing but booze and arthritis bound up in a meat suit. Her hands shook as she tried to light her cigarette. "I know you're lying to me. You fuckin' around?"

I didn't bother answering. Instead, I tried to focus on what I could, even though my heart was pounding in my ears.

"You must think I'm fuckin' stupid or somethin'. I know what you're up to. When are you going to get it through your thick skull that you ain't nothing special? You think you're going off to college like the rest of them girls? You're a fuckin' dumbass. Can't even get good enough grades to do nothing more than wait tables, you uppity bitch."

"Which is it, Mom?" I shot back, unable to stop myself. "Am I an uppity bitch or a fucking dumb-ass? Pick a lane. You're all over the place."

"Fuck you," Carla retorted, taking a long drag, wobbling on her feet. "You know what I'm saying."

"Whatever. Get out. I need to study."

Her slurred voice rang in my ears like the lyrics to a song you can't stand but can't stop singing. Now came Carla's favorite tune, the one where she blamed me for every failing in her life as if she hadn't been the architect of her own shitshow.

"I didn't want you but your dad — worthless fucker — told me he was going to marry me and I believed him. Surprise, surprise, no ring on the finger, just a screaming kid that I couldn't afford and didn't want. My life...ruined." She gestured uselessly at everything around her. "Is this the thanks I get for sacrificing everything? A fucking piece of trash whore who ain't doing nothing but giving me grief every day of her damn life."

Same story, different day but it still stung. She was a broken record. The only difference? I didn't cry anymore. "Maybe you should've kept your legs shut," I quipped, rising to shut the door in her red face. I leaned against the locked door as Carla screeched on the other side, banging with sloppy attempts to break it down but she was too drunk to do much damage, even to this flimsy excuse of a door. "Sleep it off, Carla," I muttered, returning to my bed.

I drowned her out with loud music and grabbed my notebook. I liked to write, not that I thought I was destined to be a novelist or anything but it helped to write down the things that chewed on me.

It probably wouldn't shock anyone to know that most of the pages were filled with rants about my mother. Guess you could say I had mommy issues. I'm sure I'll need therapy at some point but for now, I was coping in my own way.

What would happen after the auction? Would I be irrevocably ruined in the mental department? What was the emotional cost of something like this? Would I completely devolve in middle age? Crumpling in on myself as the dam broke holding back every memory from this time in my life?

A nervous breakdown on layaway.

Maybe.

Even if I seemed chill about the whole thing, it wasn't true. I scribbled my confession: *I'm not chill.*

I'm freaked out but this was my ticket out. As much as it made me cringe, if some rich guy wanted the privilege of taking my virginity...I guess he could have it for a shit-ton of money.

I wanted to tell my best friend, Lora. But I couldn't. The burden of my secret was no heavier than the rest I carried about my life but I always shared everything with Lora.

She knew my mom was a raging bitch and we had plans to attend college together. Unlike me, she had decent parents and they were helping her make it happen. Sometimes I watched her life from behind hungry eyes as the ugliness of envy whispered terrible things in my mother's raspy, booze-soaked voice. Why had fate dealt me such a bad hand? Babies were born innocent, right? If that's true, what had I done to deserve a mother like Carla?

Thoughts like that were a dangerous bog I tried to avoid but sometimes I was weak.

My cell phone rang and I picked it up, grateful for the distraction. *Speak of the devil.*

"Hey girl," I answered. "Shouldn't you be pricing all those collectible Barbies you have to sell on eBay? You're going to need beer money, you know. College ain't cheap."

Lora ignored my tease and said, "My mom wants to throw you a small birthday party. You think your mom would be cool with that?"

Oh yeah, my 18th birthday was coming up. I was one of the few high school seniors who hadn't hit the magic number yet. It was one of the main reasons I hadn't been able to bail on the home situation just yet. Carla had already threatened to report me as a runaway if I tried to leave. It wasn't because my mom had some long-buried maternal instinct — it was because she received social security money for me when my biological dad died and if I wasn't around, they'd cut her aid.

Bottom line...it was all about the money.

Was it any wonder I took Madame Moirai's deal? I've been taught my whole life that I was nothing but a payday.

That was the other thing about the auction, the girls had to be eighteen. Otherwise, it was kiddie porn, or something like that. Like being eighteen was any different than seventeen. I knew girls who'd become raging sluts by the time they'd hit fifteen. But let's protect the children, right? It seemed weird to be talking about cake when an hour ago I'd signed a document detailing the loss of my virginity. Still made my head spin. I returned to the conversation. "Who cares what my mom thinks. It's not as if she's going to go all Betty Crocker and bake me a cake, right?"

"Yeah, that's what I thought but my mom wanted to make sure. Chocolate?"

"Of course."

"Great. I'll let my mom know." There was a beat of silence. "So where'd you go today? I thought we were going to meet at The Drip for lattes."

No more lattes for me. No dairy. "Yeah, I had some errands to run," I answered, being purposefully vague. Even though I really wanted to tell Lora what I was up to, I knew I couldn't and I wasn't about to blow my opportunity just because I was feeling lonely and scared about a deal I'd made for myself. It was my bed, time to lay in it.

And, if I were being totally honest with myself, I was teensy bit afraid that Lora would find my decision abhorrent. I could stand a lot of things but seeing the judgment in Lora's eyes would just about kill me. I cared about her opinion because I know she loved me in the real sense.

So, yeah, I wasn't about to burden her with the knowledge. We'd been besties since junior high and even though we came from two different worlds, it'd hadn't mattered. Until now. The divide between us felt like the fucking Grand Canyon and it wasn't anyone's fault but it was there just the same.

"Are you okay?" she asked. "You seem off today."

"I have a lot on my mind." My mind picked at straws, searching for something believable. "Those financial aid packets you dropped off are seriously challenging my intellectual limits. I swear I think the government is purposefully weeding out the ones they deem unworthy by putting them through the FAFSA gauntlet."

"True story. My dad had to do mine."

Sometimes I liked to imagine that my dad, if he hadn't run off and left my pregnant mother and then gotten himself killed in a DUI a year later, might've been a decent guy once he matured. And maybe he would've been the kind of guy who would help me fill out financial aid packets.

But the reality was more like, he probably would've been a douche and just as bad as my mother because birds of a feather flocked together.

Tough game to play. But that wasn't Lora's reality. Her dad was Wally Cleaver. I faked a yawn. "I better get back to it. No one but me to figure this shit out," I told her, which was true.

"Maybe I could help?" Lora thew out there as a polite gesture but I knew she was just being nice because frankly, Lora would probably only make things worse. I loved the girl but numbers weren't her thing.

"You know I love you, right? But if you couldn't figure out your own application, I sincerely doubt you can do much better with mine. I'll take my chances with Youtube leading the way," I told her.

"You're right. I'm sorry. I'm kinda useless with that stuff."

"You're forgiven. Now, go price those dumb dolls. I wasn't joking about the beer money."

She laughed and clicked off.

I felt a million miles away from anything remotely close to anything Lora was experiencing in her life. Lora was a virgin, too, but she was saving herself for marriage. She was a hopeless romantic, which was cute.

I supported her decision because I was her best friend but sometimes I wondered if there was something deeper going on with that girl. Sometimes I caught the barest hint of a person I didn't know inhabiting my best friend's body but then she would disappear and Lora would return. Most times I thought maybe I'd imagined it. I sighed and fell back on my bed, feeling a little sick to my stomach after everything had gone down today.

I wondered if I knew of anyone else who'd taken Madame Moirai's deal. I didn't know how I'd been selected, only that I'd made the cut.

I worried my lip as I thought about the men who would bid on me. I wasn't ugly, actually, I think I was, sort of, pretty. Hard to tell when your mother always spent more time putting you down rather than lifting you up.

I rose and stood before my full-length mirror hanging on the back of my door. I was petite, barely five feet four inches — *thanks mom for the zero prenatal care and poor nutrition* — but somehow I'd been graced with big boobs and curvy hips. I was like a cartoon character. I turned and surveyed my ass — plenty of junk in that trunk — and wondered if that was something that would work in my favor or against it. Hard to tell. My hair, long and dirty blonde, was thick, at least, and probably my best asset. I turned enough heads to support the thought that I was good-looking and just thanked my lucky stars I'd been smart enough to avoid boys — and men — when they'd swarmed around me as soon as I was old enough to wear a bra.

I stripped and stood naked, eyeing myself with a critical eye until I blushed and wondered if I was up to what I'd just signed on for. I quickly pulled on an old sleep shirt and climbed into bed, wishing it was over already.

Please God, I know I probably committed a

terrible sin by selling my V card, but could you please, please, find me a buyer that isn't a total pig or some psycho who wants to wear my skin? Thank you.

I drifted into a fitful sleep, my dreams an anxious mess of faceless men with hurtful hands and leering mouths.

3

My birthday came and went — *woohoo, I was legally an adult* — and life crept on at a snail's pace as I awaited the summons. I knew it was coming soon. My cycle had finished, I was adhering to the regimen and I had a feeling the text message was coming. Maybe I had some latent psychic sense because two weeks after my birthday, my cell buzzed to life with the short instructions.

"Make arrangements. The car will come for you at 1800 hours at the meeting point tonight. Do not be late."

I typed, "okay" and then sat, shaking, realizing the time had come. No more waiting. I swallowed and rose on unsteady feet to pack the bag as instructed in my care sheet. I would be gone for five days.

I had no idea what happened in those five days, or which day the auction was held. I wasn't allowed too many details. Made sense to keep the chattel in the dark, right? The less detail, the less chance of leaking information.

Tears leaked from my eyes. I wiped away the moisture. Crying? Over what? It wasn't as if I'd been saving myself for marriage. I didn't know why I was crying but there was no mistaking the tears dribbling down my face. *Get it together, Nicole.*

I didn't have the luxury of bawling over something that meant so little. Losing your virginity hurt from what I'd heard. Some girls had it worse than others. And then some girls didn't have any pain at all. I hoped I was in the latter camp. Hopefully, it would be a breeze and my bank account would be fatter for it.

I stuffed my overnight bag and then left a note for my mother — not that she'd read it — I would be gone for a few days. It was Christmas break so I didn't have to worry about school. I left my house and took an Uber to the place where a sleek black car idled, waiting for me. I wasn't late — the car was early, which meant there was no time to get my nerves settled before climbing in.

I slid into the black leather interior and swallowed the instant attack of jittery fear that followed as the black-out windows completely obscured where we were going. For all I knew I was being shuttled to my death. I was overreacting, right? I settled against the fine leather and found a bottle of champagne cooling, along with a note: *help yourself* and I didn't hesitate even though I rarely drank. I downed a glass of the bubbly stuff and waited for it to calm my nerves.

If they were going to murder me, they wouldn't send a nice car to come get me, right? It was too late to back out but I could feel cold feet setting in as I second-guessed my decision to do something so fucked up.

Panic threatened to close my throat. In that moment I didn't feel brave or flippant about what I was about to do. All the bravado that'd carried me to this point had evaporated, leaving me a shaking, near-piss-myself mess.

We drove a long while before the car slowed to a stop. I heard a mechanical gate slide open. Gated community? I could only guess. Seeing as I'd spent a large portion of my life living in a shitty old apartment on the bad side of the city, I had no idea where the really rich people lived. And by rich, I meant anyone who could afford food and their utilities at the same time. I couldn't tell you how many times I'd sat in darkness because my mom didn't pay the bill. Sucked big time, especially when the hot water heater was dependent on the electricity.

The car stopped and the door opened. I didn't know the driver, not that it mattered. The same man who'd been with me to sign documents was waiting but my stare was focused on the giant house nestled in the countryside. We'd definitely left Manhattan. We'd come to the Taj Mahal. I couldn't help my reaction. Houses like this only existed in fiction. Or maybe Europe. I was immediately intimidated by the sheer scope of the rambling structure.

The man waited patiently as if he were accustomed to my reaction until he gestured, "Shall we?" and I remembered to close my gaping mouth and nod. Shouldering my bag, I followed him into the foyer. I was going to stay in this house? I'd never been in a house so big it had wings. And this place definitely had wings. It probably had an elevator. And a dungeon.

"Is this your house?" I asked.

"No."

Of course not. What a stupid question. "Who owns it?"

He didn't answer. Instead, he said, "Olivia will show you to your room. Further instructions will be given once you've been situated. I trust you made arrangements as instructed?"

"My mother doesn't care where I go as long as I come back eventually. Don't worry, she's not going to look for me."

"Excellent," he said and I winced. The fact that I could leave for five days and no one would notice... well, that stung. Actually, Lora would miss me. She's the one I felt bad about lying to. I told her I was going to visit a grandmother I didn't have. She bought it, only because I'd learned a long time ago how to tell a convincing lie. "Olivia, show our guest to her room."

Olivia, a young woman who looked to be about five years older than myself, dressed smartly in a black and white suit, nodded and gestured for me to follow.

The marble floor was unreal, but I supposed that you couldn't have a mansion like this and have regular ol' linoleum. I was almost afraid to walk on it for fear of leaving shoe marks from my sneakers. The pristine surroundings made me immediately self-conscious as if the stone statues guarding the stair-well were going to cover their nose at the smell of poverty that surely clung to my skin. "This will be your room. You will share it with the other guests. Lights out by eight. No exceptions. Well-rested young ladies look the freshest."

I nodded and she came into the room, showing me the amenities with brisk efficiency. There was a huge attached bathroom with a bathtub big enough to swim a few laps and everything gleamed in the light. She pointed to the folded silken nightgown and robe awaiting on the counter. "You will bathe and dress for bed. Tomorrow will be a long day of prepa-ration." Then she reached out, saying, "I'll take your bag. We will provide everything you'll need."

I hesitated. My cell phone and ID were in the bag. Olivia's expression told me there was no compromising. "Will I get it back when I leave?" I asked.

Her short smile gave me chills as she answered, "Of course."

The last thing I wanted to do was relinquish all control but it was clear I didn't have a choice. I handed over my bag and she smiled at my obedience.

Without another word, Olivia left, the sound of the lock sliding into place driving home the knowledge that there was no turning back. I was in the boat and the current was sending me downstream.

A long day of preparation...this was really happening.

I was being prepared for...my cheeks heated. Someone was going to pay to...I couldn't even say it out loud even though I'd never considered myself a prude or overly sensitive about sex. This was it.

And what kind of preparation was going to happen? What did that mean? I was almost afraid to know. Maybe ignorance was best. I returned to the bathroom and picked up the nightgown. The filmy satin whispered through my fingers. This probably cost more than I made in a year.

But God, it was fucking beautiful. Extreme wealth was another world and I was momentarily lost in wonder at the extravagance.

Usually I slept in an old ratty tee-shirt. I glanced down at myself, feeling grubby in my new surroundings. I worried my bottom lip as I surveyed the room. There were four beds in total. Olivia said more guests were coming. It wasn't a hard line to draw that guests meant girls.

Olivia said to bathe. I guess that meant I was supposed to take a lap around the tub before bed. That part I didn't mind. After a quick check on all the windows and doors and finding them locked tight as a prison ward, I closed the bathroom door and started the water. Essential oils awaited on a silver platter beside the tub. After sniffing a few, I added drops to the water, undressed and slid into the heated water.

I couldn't remember the last time I took a real bath. We only had a shower at home and the water pressure wasn't shit. If someone flushed the toilet, the water would scald your skin off. And it was filthy. No amount of scrubbing could ever get that thing clean. I finally gave up and spent as little time as possible in it. I liked showering at Lora's place. Her shower was always sparkling clean, smelled of lavender, and had the fluffiest towels I'd ever felt across my ass.

As nice as Lora's parents were, I couldn't sneak off to use their shower every day before school. I had to make do with what I had.

But this place? It was next level glamorous. I'm talking Lifestyles of the Rich and Famous level of wealth. It was awe-inspiring but it also made me feel small and out of place.

Under different circumstances...this might be nice. At least for a visit. I wasn't sure about living in a place like this. For all its beauty, there was no warmth, no sense of home. Not that my house felt like a home either. Maybe it was all the marble and stone that made the place seem hard and cold. I sank a little deeper in the water, shivering in spite of the heat lapping at my bare skin.

How many girls had Madame Moirai auctioned off? The secretive nature of the operation prevented questions but that didn't stop my mind from going there. Gran had always said my brain was too busy for my own good. Couldn't say she was wrong, either.

Thanks to the nondisclosure clause, good luck finding anyone willing to talk. The subject matter lent itself to secrecy. Who wanted to tell people what they'd done to get their money? Most people didn't shout to the rooftops all the sordid and dirty things they'd done in their life. Better to slink away, clutching your cash, all too eager to forget how you'd earned that payday.

That would be me. As soon as I left this place, I'd shove it so far from my mind it would take a crowbar to wrench open that locked door.

Five days of my life to pay for my future.

I had to keep that reminder front and center otherwise, I started to cry and the tears irritated me. I wasn't that girl who wept in the face of bad things. I stared them down and came out the victor, no matter how hard I'd been hit.

This situation was no different than anything I'd been through. If I was going to come away with scars, at least I'd leave knowing my suffering had been worth something.

I must've dozed off because I awoke with a start when I realized someone else had entered the bedroom. I heard Olivia's same instructions to the new girl and then heard the door lock again behind her. I quickly climbed from the tub and toweled off, then after dressing in the silken pajamas and robe, I ventured from the bathroom to get a look at my roommate.

I don't know what I expected but I didn't expect her.

4

I didn't mean to startle her but she nearly jumped out of her skin when I said hello.

"Sweet Jesus, don't do that. My nerves are already a mess and I about had a heart attack just now," the girl said, her hand going to her chest as if she were indeed, trying to prevent her heart from jumping out. She collected herself, then said, a little shyly, "My name's Tana...what's yours?"

Tana reminded me a tender rabbit venturing out into the world for the first time only to wander into a fox den. She didn't belong in a place like this. I'd assumed Madame Moirai's picks would be more like me — hardened by life, cynics down to their marrow — but Tana was soft and sweet, reminding me of Lora.

I was seized by panic. Tana seemed like a nice kid. She shouldn't be here.

"Cat got your tongue?" Tana teased when I hadn't answered.

"Sorry," I mumbled, trying to quell my concern for a girl I'd just met. Everyone had their own lives to live. I couldn't waste my energy worrying about a stranger who'd made her bed with the same sheets as me. "My name's Nicole."

Tana rolled my name around on her tongue, determining, "Nicole. Such a pretty name" before holding her hand out with a sunny smile. "Nice to meet you."

"Nice to meet you, too." Polite niceties seemed ridiculous given our situation but I wasn't about to snap at the girl for no reason. Our situation was shitty enough without me adding to the mess.

Tana's expression faltered as she gazed around the opulent room, clasping her hands together. "This place is real nice. Like the nicest place I've ever seen in my life. It's like a palace or something."

"Yeah, it's pretty nice," I agreed, peering at her in question, unable to stop myself even after I'd reasoned that I shouldn't poke my nose into the business of others. "So, I guess you're here for the same reason as me?"

Tana blushed so red, it nearly rivaled the flaming curls on her head. "Good God, can you believe it? I'm still in shock over the whole thing. I think I was a different person signing those papers. I've never done anything so...well, like this, you know?"

I believed her. "Me either."

"But how can you pass up such an opportunity, right?" It seemed she needed me to validate her decision so I nodded. She exhaled in relief. "Yeah, I mean, it's not that big a deal in the big scheme of things. Some girls aren't virgins by the time they're fourteen nowadays. In a way, if you think about it, we're kinda special for being chosen."

No. There was no slapping a pretty label on what was happening and I couldn't pretend it was anything other than what it was, not even for sweet, tender Tana. We were cogs in a machine bigger than us, we were one of many moving parts. Best to remember that or else we'd be crushed. "Let me guess...shitty parents?"

Tana's eyes widened as she shook her head, answering, "No, my parents died when I was a kid. My nana raised me."

"So your nana is terrible?"

"Goodness no, she's a saint. I love her with everything I have."

I frowned, truly confused. "So why are you...?"

Her green eyes welled with tears. "She has dementia. I need the money so I can help take care of her like she took care of me. I don't know what else to do. I can't get a good job without a college education and right now I can't leave her for longer than a few hours at a time. It's not her fault that she forgets things and gets confused. I can't let her down. She needs me."

That pulled at my heartstrings (I didn't realize I had those) and I felt the need to give the girl a hug. Not that I'm a big hugger by nature but it seemed the right thing to do. Tana was selling herself for a noble reason, which made my reasoning seem selfish and self-serving. I blinked back tears that came out of nowhere. "It's not going to be so bad," I said, even though I had no idea how it was going to be. "It'll be over in a pinch and then...we'll be rich enough to do what we need to do with our lives. Just think of how much better you'll feel when you no longer have to worry about money."

Tana nodded, wiping at her eyes, grateful for my kindness. "I know. I'm just not sure how I'm going to live with myself afterward. I mean, it isn't right what we're doing."

Her quiet confession poked at my own fear. "You

shouldn't have to apologize for doing what you feel is right for you," I said, refusing to feel cowed by someone else's version of morality. If there was anything I'd learned, life wasn't fair and the rules didn't apply to everyone equally. "Don't beat yourself up over doing something that's going to change your life forever. It's one night. And then, it's all over."

"What if they want more than one night?" she asked fearfully. "I don't think I can do that."

The thought hadn't occurred to me. Then, I hardened my voice as I answered with a bravery that wasn't entirely false, "Then they'll pay out the nose for each extra day."

"You're so strong," Tana said, awed. "I wish I was more like you."

"No you don't," I told her. "Try to stay sweet, Tana. Don't be like me."

The door opened and Olivia returned with another servant and two more girls trailing behind her. The servant carried more silky pajamas and handed a set to each girl as they wandered in.

I surveyed the competition — we were all competing for those top dollars, right? — and realized we were all different in looks and size but there was one thing we all must have in common...desperation.

All of us had a reason to sell ourselves and that, in itself, created a strange connection.

Olivia and her servant exited, locking the door again as they left. I turned to Tana. "Does it feel like we're prisoners in a really nice hotel?"

"Yeah, why do they lock the door? That's creeping me out," Tana answered with a tiny shiver. "It's bad enough that we're doing this in the first place, why make it worse?"

The brunette with the short, sassy hair and big golden eyes claimed the bed furthest from the door and regarded everyone with wary curiosity. "Should we do a roll call?" she ventured and I wasn't sure if that was a good idea or not. I mean, it's not as if we were all going to hold hands and sing campfire songs. Besides, I already had a best friend. But maybe it wasn't a terrible idea and I was just being a prickly bitch so I relented. "Nicole. What's yours?"

"Jillian but my friends call me Jilly."

What a perfect name for her, I thought. Perky and sweet...like a cheerleader's name. No question as to why she was picked up. She could probably do a back handspring and land in the splits right onto the guy's dick. Some guys were into that. Tough luck if my buyer hoped for something like that from me. I couldn't do a cartwheel to save my life.

Tana smiled. "That's cute. I'm Tana."

Our gaze swung collectively to the other one, a long-haired dark brunette with dazzling blue eyes who looked as friendly as a wet cat and I realized with a start I knew her. *Holy fuck.*

It'd been a long time since I'd seen her. We'd attended the same elementary school — sixth grade, I think? — back when my mom and I lived in Brownsville. For a short stint, my mom thought she was going to become a theater actress but like all of my mom's half-baked ideas, it hadn't panned out.

Of all the places to run into someone from my jigsaw past, this seemed unreal.

Her name was Dylan. I didn't remember her last name but I recognized her just the same.

Did she recognize me? Our gazes met and held. She knew. I said nothing and neither did she. I guess we were keeping that information private. Tana decided to make the first move, going to Dylan with an outstretched hand. "I'm Tana..."

Dylan ignored Tana's offer and Tana took the hint. "Okay...well, if no one minds, I think I'll take the bathroom next. I don't know what the punishment is for not bathing before bed but I don't want to find out."

I didn't blame Tana. I didn't want to know either.

Tana scooped up her pajama set and disappeared behind the bathroom door, leaving me, Jilly and Dylan behind.

I looked straight at Dylan. "Why'd you take the deal?"

"Why did you?"

"Because I have a shitty mother and I'm not going to go down with her ship. I want out and the only way to do that is to have money. This seemed the fastest way to get what I needed," I answered with blunt honesty. "Your turn."

But it was Jilly who spoke up. The girl with the obvious chip on her shoulder remained stubbornly silent. "Foster care system reject," she said, raising her hand. "Once I turned eighteen, I was turned out. The state was no longer obligated to care for me and well, I didn't much care for the deal that my last foster dad came up with, so...I bailed. Two women shelters and a group home later...I was contacted by Madame Moirai, I mean not actually Madame Moirai herself but someone working on her behalf. I took the deal because I have nowhere to go and I figured if I stayed on the streets much longer, I wouldn't have a virginity left to bargain with."

Cold truth. Streetlife was harsh.

"What was the deal your foster dad offered?"

Dylan asked. "Let me guess...he wanted to pluck your cherry, too? In return, he'd offer you room and board for services rendered?"

Jilly held Dylan's sardonic stare and nodded. "Yeah, something like that. Needless to say...I told him to fuck off."

I chuckled, agreeing with her. Sounded like something I would say, too. I didn't want to but I liked her. There was something about Jilly that made me want to smile and I wasn't easily influenced that way.

"Ironic that you're here...selling your cherry again, right?" Dylan said.

"Yeah, well, at least here I get to make the choice and I'm getting a helluva lot more than a bed and a meal."

I agreed. "One the control is taken from you, the other, you take control. They're our fucking bodies... we should be able to choose what we do with them and that includes selling them for a better opportunity."

Dylan's wry amusement rubbed me the wrong way. I cast a hard look her way. She held up her hands in mock surrender. "Whoa there, bra-burner. Calm down. I'm just saying, it's ironic."

"If you're so full of judgment, why'd you take the deal?" I asked.

"Personal reasons," Dylan stated flatly.

"Yeah, well we all have *personal* reasons," I returned with a snort. "No one signs up for this gig because they were bored one Sunday afternoon."

She glanced from me to the rest of the girls, then shared, "Same story. Daddy had wandering hands. I didn't feel like being a victim so I took the deal. Like I said, personal."

"Well, aren't you a bad-ass," I said.

"You have no idea."

Jilly chewed her lip, voicing a fear we all shared even if we didn't want to admit it. "What if our buyer isn't nice?"

"As long as they don't leave permanent marks, they have the right to be any way they want. It's in the fine print," Dylan said, swinging her legs over her bed and standing so that she could get a better look around. "I wonder who owns this place? Maybe the mysterious Madame Moirai herself. Forty percent of every girl she sells, probably earns her a pretty penny." She turned to cast a short glance our way. "Makes you wonder who this wily bitch is, doesn't it?"

Yes, it does. "Ever wonder if it's someone we all

know? I mean, how'd she know to offer us the deal? She has to have quite a network, right?" I said, wondering how Madame Moirai came across her girls. It's not as if girls wore a big V on their forehead advertising that they were virgins. "How did you get the invitation?"

"I was in a coffee shop and a runner dropped off a note, asking if I wanted to make a lot of money," Jilly chimed in with a nervous dart of her gaze. "Funny thing was, I'd just spent my last two dollars on a crappy black coffee because I was trying to get a job there and I thought it would look good if I was also a customer. So, needless to say, the idea of making a quick buck appealed to me. The note left a number to call and so I called it."

Dylan didn't share how Madame Moirai found her. Her lips remained firmly buttoned. It was becoming pretty clear Dylan wasn't a sharer by nature.

"That means whoever this Madame Moirai is... she's been watching us for quite a while, right?" I surmised, getting an all-over body creepy feeling. I didn't like the idea of being watched. "And then, you met with Mr. Personality to go over the terms, right?"

"Who is Mr. Personality?" Jilly asked.

"Just a name I gave the guy who's been the face

throughout my transaction. Dark hair and eyes, kind of a cold fish but good-looking in a generic sense? Kinda like what I imagine a sex bot would look like if it was a sentient being."

"Blech," Jilly grimaced but confirmed with a nod. "I think I talked to the same guy, too."

Dylan wondered, "I wonder who he is to her? Maybe there is no Madame Moirai. Maybe she's just a figurehead for a network of people involved in this scheme."

"Maybe. Either way, someone's getting rich," I said, taking in the sumptuous surroundings. The contents of this one-room could equal more money than I'd ever see in ten lifetimes. My mom wasn't exactly liquid in the cash department. Carla always made sure to have enough cash to buy booze but never enough to make sure there was food in the fridge.

Tana reappeared, her fair features flushed from the heat of the bath. "It's all yours, whoever's next," she said, climbing into her bed, her gaze darting between us all. "What'd I miss?"

"Just trying to unravel the mystery of Madame Moirai," I answered.

Tana shuddered. "I don't want to know."

That surprised me. "Why not?"

"Because I just want this all to end and when it's over, I don't want to think about it ever again. I don't care who she is. If I could back out...I probably would. My stomach is in knots and I'm not sure what I was thinking when I agreed to do this. We're all going to hell for selling ourselves like this," Tana said with a shiver, wrapping her arms around her knees. We were all around the same age but Tana seemed so much younger.

"Hell doesn't scare me. I've already lived there, bought a vacation home and flipped rentals in that zip code," Dylan said, adding, "But I definitely want to know who's running this show."

Tana said with absolute conviction, "That seems like information that could get you in trouble."

"Yeah, well sometimes not knowing gets you in trouble, too." With that, Dylan walked past us and disappeared into the bathroom.

The other two girls were easy enough to figure out but Dylan...she was a wild card.

Tana turned on her side, burying herself beneath the blankets. I shared a look with Jilly. We were thinking the same thing. We were all in the same boat, no matter our circumstance or how we tried to put an acceptable spin on it. The fact was, I knew how Tana felt even if I didn't let on because I felt the same way. When this was all done...I wanted to forget, too.

There were somethings that you just didn't want to talk about.

This experience would rank at the top of that list.

5

The next morning, Olivia woke us bright and early to start our preparations. We were taken into separate rooms and given massages. Even though it felt good, I couldn't shake the feeling that we were being tenderized for slaughter. We were offering up our bodies to God-Only-Knew and our skin needed to glow with youth and vitality.

My stomach clenched with nerves. I gritted my teeth against the thoughts in my head, so much so that the masseuse noticed.

"You are so tense," the masseuse remarked, lightly tapping my shoulders, her lightly accented voice gently chiding, "Relax, darling. Today you are a princess. Let us pamper you."

But I didn't feel like a princess. I felt like a prized

cow getting fancied up for the inevitable moment of being selected and purchased.

I needed a distraction. Anything to keep my mind from spinning.

"Do you always work for Madame Moirai," I asked, curious. "How many girls have you seen go through this process? A lot?"

"Shhhh, you mustn't ask questions, lovey. Just enjoy this moment. You are very special."

"Why am I special? Do you know how Madame Moirai picks her girls? I gotta tell you, the process is pretty shrouded in secrecy. Almost seems like there's something shady about all this but I'm sure every-thing is legit."

I wasn't prone to rambling but I had verbal vomit flowing from my mouth.

"So cute and petite you are," the masseuse crooned as if the compliments made me feel anything more than icky. "Everything will work out for you."

"How do you know?" I asked, trying to crane my neck to look at her but she gently pushed me back down. I settled my face in the hole with an exhale. I didn't expect the woman to answer. At least not truthfully. If I'd had to sign a nondisclosure clause, likely so did everyone else involved in this illegal operation. My mind was hard to silence though. "I won't tell anyone," I promised.

"Such supple skin," the masseuse continued as if I hadn't spoken, her hands on every part of my body. "So lucky to have such beauty."

Did she say that to all the girls? Flattery wasn't my currency. I wasn't distracted or calmed by cheap words thrown my way. If anything effusive compliments made me wary of what the person wanted. Nothing came for free. In my experience when people were buttering you up, they had a reason.

"You're very good," I said, using the woman's own tactics. "I bet Madame Moirai only hires the best."

"High standards are expected of anyone associated with the Avalon."

Avalon? What was that? "What is the Avalon?" I asked. The subtle pause in her ministrations gave away that she'd shared too much, which made me pay particular attention as I pressed a little harder. "Is it like a company or something? Like the organization that runs the auction? I never saw Avalon on any of the papers I signed."

A tiny hint of agitation flowed through her fingertips as she chastised me into silence. "Quiet now. You must relax and let me pamper you, lovey.

Next, you will be waxed. That process is less enjoyable."

Waxed? I didn't want to be waxed but I wasn't given a choice in anything. The privilege of choice was taken from me the moment I signed the deal.

Even as her fingers worked magic, my mind wouldn't settle. Too many questions crowded my brain. What the hell was the Avalon? I'd never heard of that name before. Only Madame Moirai had been on the paperwork, which obviously wasn't a real name but I hadn't pushed for too many details from Mr. Personality when I'd signed on the dotted line.

"You are finished," she said in her soft voice but before she left, she whispered, "Be pleasant and agreeable. It's the only way."

The only way for what? I pushed up from the table, trying to catch a glimpse of my masseuse but she scurried from the room before I could get a good look. *What did she mean?* I clutched the fluffy white towel to my body. What if this was a huge mistake? I sense of foreboding crawled up my arms. A pungent odor of fear and dragon's blood essential oil rising to my nostrils.

There was no escaping this place. I had to ride it out. One way or another.

Olivia came to collect me. I followed her into

another room where another person awaited. A surgical mask covered most of their face but I could tell it was another woman. At least that was something. I didn't want to be waxed by a man.

She gestured to the table. "Drop your towel. Get on the table."

The woman's clipped tone bordered on aggressive. I wasn't about to pick a fight with the woman ripping hair from my body so I smothered my urge to tell her to *fuck off* and climbed on the table.

I started to share, "I've never had—" but the woman didn't hesitate or proceed with a gentle hand. I shrieked, tears jumping to my eyes but she simply swatted my hands away when I tried to make her stop. *Holy Jesus!* Why would anyone do this willingly?

"Spread your cheeks," she intoned.

I stared in mortification. *Excuse me?* "Is that really necessary?" I asked.

"No one wants to play with a hairy anus," the woman answered as if annoyed that I'd spoken at all.

"I don't want anyone playing with my *anus*, hairy or not," I retorted, my face heating. "I didn't sign up for that."

She stared at me with impatience. "Spread your

cheeks, now or I will bring someone in to do it for you."

I swallowed, realizing I wasn't going to win. Slowly turning, I did as I was told, squeezing my eyes shut, mentally telling myself this would be over soon. As efficiently as before, she waxed the area with quick motions.

What level of hell had I signed up for?

Finished, I gratefully hopped from her table, eager to leave, only to discover another level of degradation.

The enema.

A different woman with the square body like a brick wall instructed me to lie on the table on my side. I stared at the contraption in her hand and shook my head. "Hell no. Just what do you think you're going to do with that thing?" I demanded.

"It's all part of your contract."

"I don't remember an enema being part of the fine print," I told her, glaring. "I'm not doing that."

She shrugged as if she didn't care one way or another and I realized I wasn't going to get out of it. "What's it for?" I asked, stalling.

"So that you are completely clean for the client. You will be given a clear liquid diet afterward so as to keep yourself pure."

I felt queasy. This was all for anal sex. I wasn't scared of losing my virginity but I'd never considered that the man who purchased me, would want...I felt woozy. "What if I don't want to have my butt used that way?" I asked even though I knew I would find no sympathy.

As expected, the woman just shrugged but the subtle smirk on her face told me she knew I didn't have an option. I climbed onto the table and rolled to my side, grimacing as I felt her gloved hands parting my cheeks. Good God, could this be more humiliating? I could die right then and there.

I thought of Tana. How was she handling this kind of intrusion? If I was struggling, Tana was probably a sobbing mess. *Just get through it. It'll all be over soon. Think of the money. Think of leaving with Lora to college. Think of anything but this moment.*

"You have an ass made for fucking," she said by way of observation as if that were the most common thing to say to a stranger, much less a teenager. "You'd better get right with the idea because with an ass like yours...it's going to happen." Suddenly, she must've taken pity on me because she added, "it can be pleasurable if done right. Hopefully, your buyer will be kind and be gentle so that you can enjoy, it too. Otherwise, it'll feel as if someone is pulling you apart. The pain can be excruciating."

This woman was a sadist. How could she say something so flippant to someone who was obviously nervous and scared? I hated her hands on me. I hated what she was doing. I hated everything about this degrading situation I'd signed up for.

"When is the auction?" I asked, bracing myself for the answer.

"Tonight."

Her answer chilled me. It made sense. That's why we were being prepped today. The auction loomed and I couldn't catch my breath for a moment. Again, I felt dizzy. Maybe it was because I had something up my butt already but I was nearing a freak-out level. I didn't feel like an adult who'd made a conscious decision to control my fate — I felt like a little kid who was about to get molested by a stranger.

I worried about Tana. I doubted she was handling the butt care very well. I squeezed my eyes shut and tried not to think about anything but how I was doing something that was going to better my life.

"Who is Madame Moirai?" I asked, gritting my

teeth as my stomach cramped from the warm soapy water going up my colon. "Fuck, this sucks!"

"Hold it in as long as you can," she instructed. "The longer you hold it, the better it works."

"What kind of perverts are going to be invited to this shindig?" I asked, holding my breath as I struggled to hold onto my dignity and my bowels. "This is disgusting."

"No, this is necessary for anal play or else you're going to make a terrible mess once a cock goes up there," she answered as if this wasn't the most degrading experience of my life. "Besides, it's also a safety precaution for the buyer as well. No one wants a poopy surprise."

I gagged. That wasn't going to happen. Good God, that wasn't going to happen! Tears trickled from my eyes. "I can't believe this is happening. I'm in a nightmare."

Her wry chuckle had nothing in common with kindness or understanding. If anything, there was an undercurrent of scorn as she said, "You knew what you were signing up for. Do you know how incredibly lucky you are to be chosen as a Madame Moirai offering? She's known for procuring only the best, which means you must have something special."

Special. Fuck that. I didn't want to be special

anymore. However, this was the most anyone had said to me about the process and as much as I loathed the woman with the cold hands and even colder heart, I needed a distraction. "What do you mean?" I asked through gritted teeth.

She tsked as if the answer should be obvious. "No virgin pussy by itself is worth the kind of money the buyers shell out. There has to be more than just virginity on the table. Looks, personality, there are many variables that go into the selection process."

"And how does Madame Moirai find her girls?" I asked, biting back a groan as I tried not to shit myself.

But the woman knew well enough to leave those sorts of questions unanswered as she announced briskly, "Time to flush! Use the lemon spritz afterward."

I hobbled from the table and locked myself in the bathroom and unloaded the contents of my lower intestines until I thought my insides might fall out. The pain was indescribable as I cramped and purged repeatedly until I was empty of anything.

Immediately afterward, the woman took me to the bath where the other girls were, each of them looking as drained and traumatized by the enema as I'd been. I didn't even bother covering my breasts as I climbed into the huge jacuzzi type Roman bath.

Tana and Jilly were pale, Dylan was silent.

"And I thought the waxing was going to be the worst part," I tried half-heartedly, my weak attempt to lighten the mood falling flat. No one felt like laughing. I didn't blame them.

I fought the urge to cry. I wanted to back out. I wanted to rip up the contract and run away from this nightmare. What had I gotten myself into? I saw the same question mirrored in the other girls' expressions. We were all questioning our decision to willfully sign on the dotted line for the promise of future freedom.

Madame Moirai had, indeed, picked the right girls for this disgusting transaction. She knew we were desperate enough to make a devil's bargain and that we were alone. All we had was ourselves.

Desperation was a powerful motivator but it also blinded. I should've run. I should've told someone. I should've told Mr. Personality to go fuck himself with Madame Moirai's filthy offer.

But I'd taken the deal. I felt as empty as my bowels.

Even the promise of future security seemed a hollow victory as I held myself together with a string.

In the fantasy, it was raining cash but the reality was…earning that payday was going to be a bitch.

I didn't know if I was strong enough to get through this.

I didn't know if any of us were.

Even hard-ass Dylan.

We were all scared kids about to sell our innocence.

How do you prepare for that?

That's easy — you don't.

6

Around eight o'clock a servant delivered what we would wear to the auction. Tana stared in utter shock at the clothing — two separate pieces, one was a tiny, tightly laced corset thing with a matching thong and the other a flimsy, gauzy wrap — and gasped, saying, "It's practically see-through! We'll be standing there naked!"

I had to agree but felt compelled to state the obvious. "We're here to sell ourselves. What makes you think that they're going to want to buy without seeing the goods?"

"I don't know," Tana admitted, holding the skimpy material with a panicked expression. "I thought...I don't know. I didn't think I would be practically naked."

"It's not a date," I reminded her gently. "They aren't looking to treat us to dinner and a movie. They're here for one thing."

"I don't want to do this," Tana cried softly, her eyes shining with unshed tears. "I want out."

"Don't be stupid," Dylan said sharply, drawing Tana's attention. "Don't you know what will happen to you if you breach your contract?" At Tana's slow shake of her head, Dylan answered, "Something tells me Madame Moirai isn't about to just let loose ends dangle. You have to go through with it."

"Why?" Tana dared to contradict Dylan, her wide-eyes desperate. "She can't make us do anything. We should be allowed to leave if the bidding hasn't started yet."

"You have a death wish or something? Jesus, you're fucking stupid," Dylan shot back, shaking her head.

Tana's gaze opened with fear. "What are you talking about? She can't...I mean, we're people. She wouldn't..." she looked to me for help "Would she?"

I didn't have an answer but the longer we were in this pretty prison, I got the feeling Dylan was probably right. The stakes were unbelievably high. We were cattle. A product. If the product became too much trouble, what was to stop them from eliminating the problem? I didn't want to think the worst but it was hard to ignore the warning tingle in my gut. "Just try to get through it, Tana. It'll be over soon."

"Yeah, twenty-four hours and we're done," Jilly chimed in, trying to be supportive but she was nervous, too.

Tana gulped, clutching a delicate cross necklace in her palm that she must've been hiding when Olivia took our belongings the day before. "Twenty-four hours," she repeated like a mantra. To herself, she said, "I can do this."

Dylan looked more closely at her costume. "It's not that bad," she said with a critical eye, holding up the corset, then she frowned. "Mine is different than yours." That caught my attention and I turned to see what Dylan was talking about. Her corset had nothing where the breasts were supposed to go.

"My guess is that you must have the best rack," I said, which then led me to think of what Nurse Ratchet had said to me. I held up my own get-up and saw that mine had an area cut out where my butt was supposed to go. My cheeks burned but I wasn't about to let that mess with my head. "And apparently, I have the best ass," I quipped as if I wasn't bothered at all.

Jilly examined hers and found that hers had an opening for her belly. In fact, hers wasn't so much a corset at all but a series of straps and buckles. "I might need help with this," she said in a small voice. "I have no idea how it works."

I dropped my costume (I couldn't think of anything better to call it) and went to help Jilly into hers because of the four of us, hers was the most confusing. With a fair amount of swearing, we managed to get Jilly trussed up in her outfit and she promptly wrapped herself in the gauzy covering, her cheeks blazing like the noonday sun. "It looks good," I said, trying to make her feel better.

But Tana was nearing a mental breakdown and vehemently disagreed. "Are you kidding me? Isn't it bad enough that we're doing this? Why do they have to strip us of our dignity, too!" She scooped up her costume and ran for the bathroom.

We were all thinking the same thing but only Dylan had the balls to say out loud as she gestured toward the closed bathroom door. "How'd that girl hook up with Madame Moirai? She's a prude."

"Shut up," I said, feeling protective but Dylan was right. Tana wasn't the right fit for something like this but we were all in this until the end.

"This is going to fuck her up," Jilly said, worried.

"I hope not," I said but like Jilly, I wasn't sure how Tana was going to survive this night. She was fragile, breakable. I worried this would break Tana's spirit. Tana was like Lora. Lora was still in love with the fairy tale idea of falling for her Prince Charming. I'd long since realized that Prince Charming didn't exist.

Tana's tender heart would be her downfall. I mean, no one could really accuse me of being sentimental but even I was a little sad that my first time wasn't going to happen with someone who loved me. It was going to be with someone who'd *bought* me. There was no way to pretty that up.

I dressed, secretly in shock at how the corset pushed up my generous breasts until they were practically in my face, and stared at how the thong disappeared between my hairless butt cheeks. I looked different for sure. Older. More experienced. If Lora could see me...*oh thank God, she couldn't.* Somehow I felt I could endure the shame of it all as long as Lora never knew what I'd done.

Tana emerged from the bathroom, scared and looking ready to piss herself. "I don't think I can do this," she whispered, tucking the gauzy wrap around herself tightly. "I don't know what I was thinking. This is...I feel like a whore."

"Tonight...we are whores," Dylan said, her flat tone matching the dead look in her eyes. "Don't try to make it anything other than what it is. Easier to swallow if you know what you're putting in your mouth."

Dylan was right but fuck, did she have to be such a cold-hearted bitch about it? I reached out to place a supportive hand on Tana, saying, "It's only for tonight. Just remember that."

But Tana was vibrating with fear. "You know why they did all that stuff to us? The waxing, the enema?" Tana asked in a terrified voice and I nodded. She wilted a little more. "I don't want to have butt sex. That's for perverts. What if God doesn't forgive us for what we're doing?"

"Fuck God," Dylan muttered. "He hasn't done anything for me lately why should I care?"

I was an atheist at best. I could see Dylan's point — if there was a God why would he let kids suffer and die because they had the bad luck of being born to shitty parents? — But Tana was in no way capable of handling that kind of truth right now. Dylan was being unnecessarily cruel and her next comment cemented that belief.

"I've heard that if you're not lubed up enough it

can ruin you for life. I'm talking spending the rest of your life with a colostomy bag," Dylan said.

I glared at Dylan. "Zip it, you're not helping and that's not true anyway."

"How do you know? If you're a virgin what do you know about taking it up the ass?" Dylan countered with a hard look.

"Just because I haven't had sex doesn't mean I've lived in a cave," I said, irritated. I wanted to duct tape Dylan's mouth shut. "You're making things worse just to be a dick."

But Dylan shot back, "No, you're the one not helping. You really think she's capable of surviving what's coming? She's going to come unglued and something bad is going to happen. Didn't you pay attention to the fucking contract we signed?"

The contract hadn't specifically stated that harm would befall us if we breached our contract but all signs pointed to the distinct possibility. I suppressed a shiver, stubbornly holding my position for Tana's sake. "Just stop. No one needs to hear that right now."

"Whatever. It's your funeral," Dylan said.

Turning to Tana, I steadied her by the shoulders, meeting her frantic gaze. "It's one night," I reminded her in a low, soothing tone. "Anyone can get through one night and then you can hire the best therapist you can find if you need to."

Tana nodded and wiped at her eyes. "One night," she repeated as a mantra. Nodding, she said in a shaky voice, "I can do this."

"Yes, you can," I agreed but I had my doubts. I had a soft spot growing for the kid. I hoped what I was said was true. I didn't want to have anal sex either but I had to prepare myself for the possibility. "Maybe your buyer won't be into that. It's not a given. They just like to cover all their bases," I told Tana, although who knew if it were true. For all I knew, anal sex was fully expected. "It's going to be okay. Just think of all the money you're going to earn and how it's going to help your nana."

Jilly smiled, her bright eyes softening. "You're doing this for your nana? Aww, that's so sweet. She must really mean a lot to you."

Tana nodded and sat heavily on the edge of her bed. "She's the sweetest, kindest person in the world. If it weren't for her, I don't know where I'd be. I have to help her." She revealed the hidden pendant. "This was from her. I know I wasn't supposed to but I brought it with me. It's probably stupid but I'm hoping it gives me strength."

I caught Dylan's subtle eye-roll but Tana didn't.

Let's be honest, we were all jealous of Tana's relationship with her nana. What if we'd had someone who cared about us in our lives? How would things have changed? The only reason Tana was here was because of a cruel twist of fate that stole her nana's brain function. Otherwise, Tana might've moved into the next phase of her life without a hiccup.

"I think that's really sweet," I said, ignoring Dylan. "You hold onto whatever helps get you through this."

Tana nodded, her eyes wide like that of a child being fed to a fire. "It's not fair," she said, running the wrap edges through her fingertips. "Why do women have to go through stuff like this?"

"Because life's not fair," Dylan answered, sounding bored. "Why did my mother run off and leave me with an asshole father who couldn't seem to keep his hands to himself? I spent so much time running away I should've joined track and at least gotten a medal out of all the miles I logged. Life's not fucking fair, princess. If you haven't learned that by now, you're either dumb as you look or you're just in over your head and about to get a real education."

"Stop it," I growled but before I could say anything more, we all heard Olivia's heels clicking down the hall toward our door. My jittery nerves returned and brought with them, psychotic butter-flies for my stomach. "She's coming."

Olivia appeared, holding a tray with four glasses of water, which she promptly handed to us before she reached into her pocket and pulled out four pills, saying, "To ease your nerves."

Tana stiffened in alarm, saying, "I don't take drugs," and Oliva put the pill in her hand with a practiced smile. Tana glared as she curled her palm around the pill. "You can't make me take drugs."

"No," Olivia agreed but added, "however, if I may suggest, do yourself a favor and take the pill. I will return in thirty minutes."

Olivia exited, leaving us to consider Olivia's advice. I detested anything that took away my ability to remain in control. Even though I wished I could just down the pill and be done with it, I knew I wouldn't. Come what may, I wanted to be sober. Although I couldn't say the same idea was a good one for Tana. She was a mess. "It's probably a Xanax," I told her, trying to make her feel better. "They wouldn't give you anything that would knock you out completely. No one wants an unconscious lay, you know?"

"Down the hatch," Dylan said, tossing the pill

down her throat and washing it down with an exaggerated smile. "Let's get this party started."

Jilly shared an uncertain look with me and reluctantly took her pill, too. "Here goes nothing," she said. "See you on the other side."

"My nana takes a Xanax now and then," Tana said, seeming to soften her stance. "I guess it's not too bad, then." She popped the pill and washed it down with a generous swallow of water. She looked to me. "You're not going to take yours?"

"My mom's a raging alcoholic and I don't want to do anything that will tip the scales toward awakening that gene hiding in my DNA, you know what I mean?"

"Oh, that makes sense," Tana agreed with a solemn nod. "You're very smart."

"Yeah, a fucking genius," Dylan quipped before adding with a damnable smirk that I was beginning to hate, "Can't fight your DNA, sugar. No matter how hard you try. What you hate, you'll eventually become."

Fuck her, she didn't know anything about me or my life. I would never be like my mother. Ever.

Holding Dylan's gaze, I deliberately tossed the pill in the trash but drank the water because my mouth was dry as dirt.

Thirty minutes later, Tana was a sweet, complacent little dove, Dylan's quips had lost their edge and Jilly clung to a sad silence. I was still sharp as a knife and scared out of my mind but I didn't regret trashing the pill.

I signed up for this, I would take whatever was coming.

7

As I imagined, the mansion had an elevator and we were being taken straight down to a sub-basement level. Hard to hold clandestine sex auctions on the ground floor, right? What would the neighbors think?

My stomach muscles were clenched tight as a fist as we followed Olivia down a darkened hallway and into a circular room with two-way mirrors on the walls and chains dangling from the ceiling.

I stared with growing apprehension as I realized we were supposed to be hung, spread-eagle as part of the show. I looked to Olivia with a mixture of HELL NO and HELP ME in my expression and she met my fear with a smile, murmuring, "You should've taken the pill."

I'd never hated anyone more than I hated Olivia in that moment. Maybe even more than the mysterious Madame Moirai because it was Olivia feeding us to the wolves with a smile.

She snapped her fingers and doors opened with strong, hard-faced, bare-chested men striding in to rip the gauzy covering from our bodies, leaving us in our corsets and little else. Then, our wrists were put in the manacles and our ankles in restraints.

It was horrifying and over-the-top with every detail designed to appeal to the sordid nature of the transaction. That this kind of thing happened beneath the noses of ordinary people going about their busy lives, ignorant to the scum seething behind the curtain of polite society was numbing.

No one cared about girls like us, which was why we were easy pickings. Every single one of us dangling like caught fish on a line were expendable. No one would truly miss us. If we disappeared, who would cry at our funeral? Hell, who would even look for us?

Lora would cry for me but she wasn't a fighter. She wouldn't crusade for vengeance. I choked on the reality that I'd put myself in a bear trap, willingly walked right up to the sharp jaws and offered my foot without thinking how much it was going to hurt when it clamped down on the bone.

Olivia was right — I should've taken the pill. DNA be damned, I should've downed the drug to spare myself the agony of clarity.

I strained against the pull on my arms, sweat beginning to dot my hairline. I changed my mind. I didn't want to do this! But there was no turning back. I couldn't if I tried. I glanced over at Tana and she was struggling weakly against her bonds but otherwise, she was too doped up to care.

Oh Tana, I wanted to cry but there was nothing I could do to help. Tears stung my eyes but I held them back. The searing pain in my wrists added an additional layer of seasoning to my fear.

Jilly hung like a tightly bound piece of meat, all trussed up like a Christmas turkey. She stared blankly at the dim mirror. Wherever Jilly was, she wasn't in this room any longer. Maybe that was a blessing. I craned my neck to see Dylan, a defiant light still gleaming in her eyes even as drugged as she was.

Dylan, doped and roped, still had the where-withal to say 'Fuck you' with her eyes even as she dangled. I envied the strength of her spirit, how she stared into the face of the unknown and dared a motherfucker to try and fuck with her. If nothing else, Dylan was a survivor.

Her spirit, however sharp and jagged, spoke to mine even if I didn't want this kind of connection with her.

Disassociating was the only way to get through this hell. Dylan really did have a great rack, her breasts, lifted high, were on display, like an offering and I looked away when I couldn't handle another minute of watching was happening to us.

I put up a good front but inside I was a quivering ball of fear and, if I'd had any food in me, diarrhea. Maybe that was the real reason they'd given us enemas. I squeezed my eyes shut, trying to be somewhere else in my mind but there was no denying that I was hung like a human side of beef, waiting to be slaughtered.

I tried to hide my trembling. I didn't want them to see that I was afraid. I would count that as a small but important victory. I had made this choice and it would be worth it, no matter what I had to endure.

Remember the nights of going hungry. Remember the time Carla left you for three days without food or running water when you were eight. Remember having to lock your bedroom door at night to keep her boyfriends from coming in when she was passed out drunk.

There were so many reasons I could pull from my memory why this had been the choice I took. Money was the greatest evil but ironically, it was also the way out of hell.

Fuck anyone who said money didn't solve problems. Soon enough I'd have enough money to forget all about this awful experience. I'd bury this memory so far down in my brain that it would take a scalpel to dig it out.

When I had that cash in my hand, I'd run so far and so fast away from Carla that my shoes caught fire.

I would never go back to my mother. She could rot and die for all I cared. I wanted to go to college and make something of myself. The satisfaction of knowing I'd risen above every attempt Carla had made to drag me down to her level was the fuel to my fire.

I'd wash the stain of my childhood away with the waterfall of money that gave me a chance to change my fate. I knew the statistics. Kids like me, with terrible foundations, didn't stray far from their roots. If chaos was all you knew, chaos was what you sought. It's why kids of addicted parents usually became addicts of some kind, too. I was hyper-aware of the pitfalls waiting for me but I was violently opposed to falling in the same hole Carla was stuck in.

I swear to Christ, that won't be me.

One and done, I told myself.

Everyone had skeletons. So mine danced naked for leering rich guys. *Don't judge.*

Tana whimpered and I knew she was going to have a hard time with things, even doped up. I worried she might break her contract after all. Irrational anger colored my thoughts as I judged the poor girl just like Dylan had.

Tana, why did you sign up for this? For fuck's sake, this is going to destroy you.

We were all stupid girls for taking the bait but we were truly trapped by our own hand and we had no one to blame but ourselves.

If Tana had thought she'd come out of this unscathed, she'd been desperately naive. I hadn't lied to myself like that. I knew whatever happened this night would leave a mark I would wear forever. No one else had to know and they wouldn't. I'd carry my shame to my grave. It was mine and mine alone.

A sultry voice sounded over the speakers and I wondered if it was the mysterious Madame Moirai, the one who was deviously and cleverly selling girls' virginity for a hefty sum to willing buyers. A person had to be soulless to do this kind of thing. Did she spend a second thinking about the girls she destroyed? Did she lose a moment's sleep wondering about the aftermath?

I knew the answer even if I didn't know Madame Moirai. Fuck no, she didn't give two shits about us. We were commodities to buy and sell. End of story.

I needed to focus on something, anything other than the voice over the speaker listing my attributes. I winced and closed my eyes, imagining myself someplace else. A beach, a forest, a college campus, anywhere but here.

"Smooth skin like alabaster, not a single blemish, tight, firm stomach, and the sweetest ass made for pleasure. Spirited and smart, taking this treasure is something you will remember above the rest. The bidding will start at fifty thousand."

I nearly swallowed my tongue. Fifty thousand? Holy shit. Who the hell had that kind of money lying around for the privilege of breaking in a cherry? I hadn't thought in my wildest dreams that I would command that kind of cash.

I'd never felt more dirty in my life and I hadn't even done anything yet.

What if it wasn't for one night as promised? A fine sheen of sweat gathered beneath my breasts. Maybe they were dishing out the cash for a permanent sex slave. Would I end up shackled to someone's bed for the rest of my life?

No, I signed a contract for five days. That was the deal. Five days. I could handle it. *Don't panic.*

The woman's voice upped the ante. I was up to sixty-five thousand. Seventy. Horror mixed with morbid fascination. Someone wanted me so bad that they'd pay huge sums of money to get their hands on me. No one in my life had ever wanted me. Why did it have to be like this? Wasn't I more than just my body?

Not to the faceless bidder behind the glass.

"Sold for one hundred and fifty thousand. Sir, you may claim your prize."

And like that it was over. I'd been sold. Someone had purchased my body and would use me as they saw fit. I wanted to puke. I wanted to scream at the asshole who thought I was nothing but a product but I bit my tongue nearly in half because the game was dangerous and there were penalties for breaking the rules.

The bidding began on Tana just as the muscle men came to collect me. To my embarrassment, my knees buckled. One of the men caught me easily, lifting me as if I were nothing to carry me from the bidding room. "Careful," he said as if he were accustomed to this happening. "No bruises before delivery."

I shuddered in disgust but remained silent as he carried me out.

The last thing I saw was Tana being undressed, displayed naked. I thanked my stars that for whatever reason, I'd been allowed to remain in my corset. Something told me, Tana wouldn't leave this experience without being irrevocably changed.

The minute we signed the document, everything about our lives changed.

I was naive to think I could do this without dying a little inside. I thought I knew what I could handle. Sex was just sex. Who cared? If some rich asshole wanted to play at being a lord, buying a woman for his own games, he could pay me. I could handle it.

How could I have been so wrong? This was hell. I'd never known such terror in all my life. Considering my childhood with Carla, that was saying a lot.

I wanted to run from this place and never look back.

But running wasn't an option. The only option

was to go through with the deal and then forget it ever happened.

Think of the money. Think of how you'll never again have to listen to Carla calling you a whore for no reason aside from the jealousy eating her alive.

I'd never been one to pray, especially since prayer had never saved me before but I found my lips moving in a silent plea to whatever higher power might be lurking in the heavens, staring down at the scene below.

I'd brought this on myself but logic worked no gears in the panicked section of my brain. I was shaking with pure terror and wishing I could turn back time to never sign the deal.

But time was up. We had to play the parts we were assigned. No matter what this night brought.

Just survive, I prayed for Tana and for myself.

Hell, for all of us. Even that bitch Dylan. *Survive.*

8

I was quickly robed in a black hooded cloak that covered me from head to toe and I was whisked away into an awaiting black car. I spun around to peer out of the darkened windows but I couldn't see anything. I turned back around to realize with a start I wasn't alone.

In the dim light, a man sat watching me. It was creepy and unnerving. I pulled the cloak around me more tightly.

Everything about him commanded power and respect. Instantly, I felt like a child and I scooted as far from him as I could manage. Was he going to maul me right here in the backseat of his fancy car? Something told me he wouldn't, but I sensed a dangerous vibe about him.

"Hello Nicole," he said, though he pronounced my name like NEE-cole and I knew he wasn't American even though I couldn't see his features very well. "Remove your cloak," he commanded.

I hesitated. I was only wearing that corset and thong. "I'm cold," I said, trying to stall.

"I will warm you."

"Are you going to hurt me?" I asked, almost desperate with anxiety.

"Only if you do not remove your cloak," he answered.

I swallowed the lump of fear in my throat and removed my cloak with trembling fingers. His eyes lit up with open appreciation and his approving smile made me want to jump from the moving car. "Come to me."

I inched my way toward him and he patted his lap. I stared. "You want me to sit on your lap? That's weird. I don't even know your name."

His gaze narrowed. "I do not give second chances, Nicole. Do as you're told and you will be rewarded. Fight me and you will be punished. You are mine — bought and paid for — I trust you understand the terms of our arrangement?"

I couldn't stop shaking but I forced a note of

bravado into my voice as I answered, "Of course, I do."

"Then come to me now and we will start fresh."

What choice did I have? I made my way to his lap and gingerly straddled him. He smiled, his hands filling with my behind. I stiffened as his fingers ran down the seam of my cheeks lightly, probing gently.

He ignored my immediate stiffening as if it didn't matter to him that his touch made my skin crawl. "You may call me Henri," he said with a short incline of his head. Perhaps he was French? His accent seemed European to me. He fixed his gaze on me. "Say my name."

"H-Henri," I repeated, uncomfortable.

"Tell me what you fear."

Where did I start? "I'm afraid it will hurt."

His smile made me think of a shark. "Pain is temporary."

"Yeah well, I'm not into pain."

"You don't know what you're into," he reminded me, his fingers squeezing me. My breath caught with fear and he slowly softened his grip, pleased with my reaction. A certain expression of benevolence softened his voice as he said, "Fortunately for you, I'm a skilled teacher" but I didn't trust him. A man who bought his lovers wasn't a good person, even if on the surface he seemed less of a monster than I feared. I didn't think for a second that I'd lucked out with a kind man.

"Why do you do this?" I asked.

"Why do I do what?" he returned, his gaze roaming my breasts and dipping lower.

"Buy young women."

He squeezed my butt in warning. "You have a sassy mouth. I will enjoy it on my cock."

I tried not to wince. What could I expect? Flowers and sweet words? No. I was bought for a single purpose. My face heated and I was grateful for the low lighting.

"Tell me why you were willing to sell your virginity. I wish to know more about you."

I paused, not sure if being starkly honest about my situation was on the table. He could have my body but did I want to share something even more intimate? I shifted and he moved one hand from my ass cheek to my front, gently petting me through the thin silk of my thong.

I froze at the first flutter of pleasure that seemed like a betrayal by my own body. I didn't consider the possibility that I might enjoy anything that would happen this night. Pain was easier to vilify.

"I wish to know you," he murmured.

I didn't want him to know me, not the real me. I resented his fingers, drumming up tendrils of pleasure that I wanted to smother. "I can't think when you do that," I admitted, embarrassed. When he didn't stop, enjoying my discomfort, I blurted out, "I needed the money" if only to get him to stop.

"You are a beautiful girl. Why have you allowed no boys to fuck you yet?"

I blushed, hating the forced intimacy of this moment. "I didn't want to risk getting p-pregnant or getting some disease for a fuck that lasted all of two minutes." I gritted my teeth against the unwelcome pleasure he created.

"Smart girl."

Not so smart. I was here, on the lap of a stranger for the most obscene of reasons. I'd call that pretty dumb in light of recent events.

"Do you fear me?" he asked with a deceptively gentle voice. *Don't buy into the facade*, I warned myself. The night was still young. Some monsters didn't show their true colors until later.

It was convenient that honesty rode side by side with the answer I knew he wanted. I nodded, waiting for his next move.

Henri abruptly stopped petting me and slapped my ass with a curt, "Off." More than happy to comply, I scooted away, covering my breasts with my arms. He gestured. "You may put your cloak back on. We're near to our destination."

He straightened his suit jacket and tie as the car rolled to a smooth stop. Seconds later the door opened. He exited the car with the expectation that I would follow.

A mansion loomed against the moonlight as demure garden lights peeped from beneath manicured hedges and rose bushes.

Did he even notice the beauty all around him or was he jaded to his privilege?

We walked briskly through the front doors into a massive foyer with inlaid marble, much like the mansion that'd held the auction. I didn't have time to admire the sheer opulence. His quick stride required hurried steps to keep up as he took me to a room off a corridor that spiked off to the left.

He breezed through the large double doors and once I had followed, he closed and locked the door behind us. Was this his bedroom? There was definitely a bed in the room but it was filled with plenty of other things that didn't involve sleeping.

Was this his...*deflowering* room? I didn't know what else to call it. Did it matter? It was abhorrent no matter the fancy features and likely imported furniture. All I saw was an overindulged dick, flaunting his wealth. I wasn't so easily impressed by shit like that.

He snapped his fingers and gestured for me to lose the cloak. I did as I was told, feeling more vulnerable than ever. What now?

He went to the bar and poured two glasses of champagne. Even though I'd taken a sip of champagne the other day, I lied and said, "I don't drink," stiffening against the offer. I didn't want him to think I was willing to get drunk with him. "My mother is an alcoholic and I don't want to be like her."

"Fair enough," he conceded, allowing me this refusal. He sipped at his own glass, regarding me with interest. Now that we were no longer in the darkened car, I could fully see him. His fine features were almost aristocratic but definitely not pretty-boy prissy. He was tall and broad. His darkened skin spoke of holidays in the Caymans or some other exotic place that I could only dream of. A full head of black wavy hair was perfectly styled with careful attention.

But for all his physical attraction, there was a dark vibe about him that kept me on guard. Maybe it was my internal bias that good people didn't buy other human beings that was setting me off but I couldn't see anything but a deviant.

I fidgeted, uncomfortable with the silence. "So now what?" I asked, wanting to get this spectacle over with so I could, possibly, go home. "Should I lay on the bed? How does this work? I've never been bought like a piece of meat so I'm not sure of the protocol," I said, unable to keep the subtle contempt from my tone. Fuck. I was going to end up dead if I didn't watch my mouth. "I'm sorry. I'm nervous," I said, trying to seem contrite.

Henri smiled but his eyes remained hard and speculative. "You are unlike most of the girls Madame Moirai procures. You are different."

I swallowed. What did that mean? "How so?" I suppressed a jump when he moved toward me. I fisted my hands, standing very still, waiting to be touched, knowing my skin would crawl with revulsion.

"You are intelligent," he answered, walking behind me with slow, deliberate steps, stopping to unlace my corset. As much as I hated the stupid thing that was nearly cutting me in half, I suddenly wanted to clutch the thing to me. "And stubborn."

If he thought I was different, that must mean he's done this sort of thing before. "How many times have you bought a girl from Madame Moirai?" I asked, licking my lips, wishing I had water to drink. "I mean, do you do this often?"

"I do it when it pleases me," he answered, the ribbon slithering free from his fingers. "But I am not often compelled to purchase as I was with you. There was something about you...something that I knew I had to have." The corset fell free and dropped to the floor, leaving me in the thong and nothing else.

I immediately covered my breasts but he stopped me, reaching from behind me to pull my arms to my side. He slowly turned me so that I faced him. He tested the weight of my full breasts with open admiration. "You have glorious tits, Nicole." He pinched a nipple and I gasped, causing the other to harden immediately. "So responsive." He bent down to suck a tight nipple into his mouth and my knees nearly gave out on me. He chuckled as he returned upright, a hungry light in his eyes. He walked slowly around me, inspecting every inch of his purchase, his fingers blazing a trail wherever he touched. "Tell me what sexual experiences you've had in your life," he said.

"None. Isn't that the point?"

"Have you not touched yourself?"

I gritted my teeth as I answered, lifting my chin

in spite of my mortification. "Sometimes."

"And did you come?"

"Y-yes."

"Good."

Fuck his approval. I listened with barely contained contempt as he went on to explain as if I were a student and he was a professor. "A woman should always know her own body. She cannot experience the full range of her pleasure if she doesn't know how to reach it on her own. However, it pleases me that you are a virgin in all ways, including the most important."

I didn't want to be schooled by this man. His arrogance was nauseating.

"Why do you like virgins so much?" I dared. Maybe I wasn't supposed to ask so many questions but I wasn't capable of just standing there like some empty-headed sex-bot.

"I find the idea of being the first between a woman's thighs stimulating. There is something so powerful and primal about being the one to introduce a woman into the world of pleasure. I crave that power and I have the means so I avail myself to it."

Even if the woman didn't have much of a choice? "I guess if you have enough money, there's nothing you can't have, right?"

His lips tipped in a cool smile as he said, "Correct."

Stopping in front of me, everything about him hardened and the change scared me. The veneer of the gracious billionaire was unlikely to be genuine. Nice people didn't buy girls. I sensed this man liked to play, which made him even more dangerous because I didn't know the rules of his game. "Undress me," he commanded.

I reached with shaking fingers to undo his tie, fumbling with the buttons of his dress shirt until I exposed his skin. Black hair fuzzed his chest and crinkled beneath my fingertips. He was so far from a boy that I could only stare for a moment.

"Do you like what you see?" he asked and I didn't know how to respond.

No, I didn't like what I saw. I didn't want to be here. I didn't want to do this.

He was undeniably attractive, a fact that I resented. It would've been easier to stomach if he'd been a bloated old toad with a stomach that hung over his waist and threatened to obscure his dick.

But that wasn't the case with Henri. His body was hard with muscle poured over bone. I wanted to puke at the sight of his obviously adult male body.

"You wear your emotions," he warned in a soft

tone, waiting for me to move to his pants. "It could get you in trouble."

"So I've been told," I answered, unbuckling his belt and unfastening the smooth button. What the fuck was I supposed to do now? I had no experience with seduction. He stepped out of his pooled pants, naked.

I averted my gaze from the protruding erection. I felt sick to my stomach.

He captured my face with both hands, drawing me to him. His lips brushed across mine in a gentle kiss that contradicted the cold and businesslike nature of our arrangement. His tongue swept my mouth, tasting. I closed off my mind, going somewhere else.

When his tongue searched for mine, I responded. His touch became more insistent as his hands pulled me closer. He groaned against my mouth and I trembled, stomping on the tiny tendrils of pleasure that dared to rise at his expert handling.

He kissed like a man who'd invented the concept of Frenching.

This man would take me tonight.

I told myself it was just my body.

But something told me, he would always own a piece of my soul and that just wasn't right.

9

I lay stunned. The wetness between my thighs a reminder of what'd happened. He hadn't used a condom – I was given a temporary birth control injection, another of Madame Moirai's protocols — and one of the reasons for the all bloodwork to ensure I was clean.

I hated the intimacy of our skin touching without a barrier. Not that latex would've done anything for the assault on my dignity.

Henri sighed and rolled from the bed to grab two water bottles. He returned and handed one to me, another flash of kindness from the considerate billionaire that I knew to be false. I accepted it, drinking deeply but nothing would wash the taste of him from my mouth.

The act itself had been nothing I wanted to remember but I felt numb inside. I hadn't thought this through. There was no amount of money that would compensate for how I felt in my soul. I drew a deep breath, trying to steady my frantic heartbeat. I wanted to wail at the world, at God, at the devil — anyone and anything I could blame for the unfair hand I'd been dealt.

All of it was overwhelming.

The pain of being entered for the first time. The degradation of feeling a man I didn't love or even know grunting above me. The crippling sadness of knowing that I would always remember this moment no matter how hard I tried to forget.

And Henri, the generically handsome yet hollow-souled john, made me want to claw his eyes out for being exactly who he was — oblivious to the cost of his entertainment.

Henri seemed curious as he returned to the bed, casually trailing his finger down my shoulder. When I moved away, he frowned. "Why do you hate me?" he asked, his eyes soft with satisfaction, content to rest while he caught his breath. "Have I hurt you in any way? First times can be difficult."

Hurt me? In ways he couldn't fathom that had nothing to do with the physical act of sex. I cut a sharp look his way but remained silent. Henri had a deceptive dangerousness about him that rippled like a heatwave and I didn't want to get burned.

"You are so quiet. I wish to know your mind. Please, you may speak freely."

I didn't believe him. "Do you expect me to be honest?" I replied, meeting his gaze with a bold stare. "You've already warned me that my emotions could get me in trouble."

"Indeed. However, I'm feeling generous. Speak your mind."

I once watched a nature documentary on TV about the King cobra charmers of India. They didn't actually charm the snake into not striking. The snake was swaying, watching the person's movement, tracking every move as it would a predator. In this particular show, the charmer had removed the snake's venom glands so there was no real danger of being bitten but an assistant had unknowingly placed the wrong snake in the basket before the show — one that was fully capable of killing a man with one strike. Misplaced confidence was the snake charmer's undoing.

He died.

Henri was the snake rising from the ornate basket, trying to convince me that he was harmless when I knew differently. Anyone who would do business with Madame Moirai was touched by evil in some way.

He nodded, giving me permission to speak freely with a magnanimous wave of his hand. "You intrigue me. Most girls are desperate to please. You are not that way. I am not accustomed to being treated like the enemy. I haven't decided if I like it or not."

Did he think I should be thankful? Maybe other girls were happy to scrape and beg and bend over backward to be someone's sex toy but I wasn't that person. I was angry. Angry at myself for agreeing to do something so disgusting. Angry at him for being the kind of person who would buy a desperate young woman. Angry at my body for feeling anything but revulsion as he sweated on top of me.

As much as I shied away from the truth, I couldn't deny that some of it had felt good even if I didn't want it to. I wanted to peel my skin off to escape the memory of his touch.

And if I was feeling this way, I could only imagine how Tana was feeling. I hoped she wasn't screaming her head off or worse, crying in a corner.

Shame curdled my guts.

But to his way of thinking, I had no reason to feel anything negative. I should feel gratitude.

And that just pissed me off.

"Decent people don't buy women," I finally said.

"Decent people do not sell themselves," he countered with a small smile. "Tell me, were you coerced to take the deal Madame Moirai offered you?"

"No."

"Were you threatened with violence if you did not agree to the terms?"

No."

He shrugged, concluding, "Then you came willingly and consensually and you will be paid for your participation. I do not see a problem. If anything, it's simply a business transaction between consenting adults."

I didn't feel like an adult when I was signing the paperwork. If anything, I felt more like a child than ever before. I couldn't have possibly known what I was getting myself into. I believe Madame Moirai banked on that ignorance to lure the girls into her circle, which made the deal all the more horrid.

"I may not have been forced physically but sometimes people know how to manipulate a situation to their advantage. My life is a shitshow. Somehow Madame Moirai had known that I would do anything to get out. Even sell myself to a stranger."

"Everyone has a price," he said, unimpressed. "Do you always play the victim?"

I stiffened. "I am not a victim."

"You sound like one. Crying over something that only has value because I gave it value. I was not cruel. I did not mark your skin or degrade you as I could have. You should be happy that I was kind and considerate of your inexperience. The only rule for the buyer is the girl must be returned *alive* to Madame Moirai's care. It says nothing about how the girl is used or the condition in which she is returned."

"You don't see how that's horrifying?"

His blank stare was answer enough. Why should he concern himself with the troubles of ants beneath his feet?

Fuck you. The conceit was enough to choke a horse. I read somewhere that the extremely wealthy had zero ability to relate to ordinary people. Henri was proof of that theory. "Were you born rich?" I asked.

"Yes."

Shocker. "Do you know who Madame Moirai is?"

"Why should I?"

His negligent answer was proof enough that he

didn't care where she got her product because we didn't have real value. Was Henri a father? Would he offer up his loved ones to Madame Moirai to be used? Of course not. They were elevated above those who scrabbled and scraped together a meager living just to survive. By that way of thinking, no wonder people like Henri thought they were being generous as they threw cash at vulnerable girls desperate for a new life. God, how I fucking loathed him and everyone like him.

I tried a different tactic. "I would think a man of your stature would be very interested in the person you're doing business with," I said. "How do you know Madame Moirai can be trusted? Prostitution is still illegal, no matter how you dress it up."

His gaze narrowed as his nostrils flared, the first sign that I'd kicked a nerve. "I know enough to satisfy my concerns and protect my interests."

"And do those interests include a family? Are you married? Kids? You're old enough to have a daughter my age. Would you offer up your flesh and blood to Madame Moirai?"

"Why are you trying to goad me?" he asked.

"I'm not."

"Lies do not suit you, Nicole," he chided.

"I'm not the one lying," I returned, holding my

breath. I was playing a very dangerous game. If I were smart, I'd shut my mouth but I couldn't. I'd never been able to bite my tongue hard enough when it mattered most. Why should this be any different? "So, would you be willing to offer up your blood to your rich friends to use as they saw fit? I mean, as long as they're returned *alive*, it should be fine, right?"

"You needn't worry about my children."

The subtle chill in his voice crawled across my skin, causing goosebumps to pucker.

"Are you a cruel man?" I pressed, ignoring his warning.

"Aren't we all capable of cruelty?" he replied, his gaze resting on my breasts. I shifted with discomfort, hoping he wasn't interested in touching me again. "And cruelty is subjective. What you may find cruel, I find a necessity. It's an endless cycle of circular logic that bores me." He moved to pull me to him. "What doesn't bore me, is your body. I could spend days discovering your hidden treasures."

"The contract is specific. Twenty-four hours," I said, my voice shaking a little. "You have to return me within twenty-four hours."

"Aren't rules meant to be broken?" Henri shifted and his erection pressed against me. I stilled, afraid to move, afraid to encourage anything but he forced my hips to rub against him. "You are a curious little bird, aren't you? So many questions. I find your mind incredibly sexy. You're much more clever than most of Madame Moirai's selections."

What did that mean? It didn't feel like a compliment coming out of his accented mouth. I tried to stop him, staring hard as I said, "What if I told you that I didn't want to do this? That I found you repulsive?"

He laughed. "Then I would call you a liar as your body tells me differently."

I couldn't control physiology. Pleasure created ripples that cascaded down the nerve endings, activating certain reactions that I couldn't control. "You're a terrible person," I said, blinking back tears.

His laughter told me he didn't give a shit what I thought. He rolled me to my back, staring down at me. Henri's smile faded as he regarded me with lust burning in his eyes. "You want me to play the part of the monster so you can feel better about your choice?"

"Yes." I wanted to hate him and everything he stood for. I didn't want to remember his touch gentle or kind because it was a lie. He played the part of the compassionate lover because playing a role appealed to him, not because it was real. Except I refused to play my role of the wide-eyed ingenue being seduced by the older, more sophisticated gentleman. I saw him for what he was: a deviant.

"Very well, little bird."

With rough hands, he flipped me to my stomach. I gasped in fear as his touch became mean and insensitive. Fingers dug into my skin as he jerked me to my knees, forcing my head down. "You should be careful what you ask for," he said in a silky tone that scared me spitless. "You have no idea what a monster I can be."

The first ring of truth from his mouth since he bought me but I knew I shouldn't have pushed so hard.

I cried out as he reached down to wrench my hair, twisting my neck painfully. I was much smaller than him. His body covered mine easily. Without care or interest in my comfort, he rammed himself inside me. I screamed, feeling ripped apart. I sobbed against the silken bedding, my fingers clutching and squeezing, trying to escape but Henri was everywhere.

"You like to play the victim, little bird? Let me give you something to cry about, something to remember so that when you put me in the role of the villain, I have truly earned the title."

"Please stop," I cried, my voice choked by tears but he was beyond hearing me.

The pain lessened as my body acclimated to the invasion but my mind was screaming. I shouldn't have provoked him. How stupid was I to play a game with someone who held all the cards? I should've played the part of the simpering sex toy, plying him with flattery and sucking his dick like it was a privilege to do so.

Stupidly, I let my mouth override my ass and wrote a check I couldn't cover. I bit my lip to keep from begging. I was still that naive girl who thought a sharp tongue could protect her from the worst life had to offer.

I wasn't prepared for Henri's world where human life could be bought and sold.

I tried to be somewhere else, to block out the reality of what was happening but it was impossible. Tears dribbled down my cheeks as I gritted my teeth against the assault, just praying he finished quickly.

After what seemed an eternity, he ended with a rattling groan, withdrawing and pushing me away. I curled up in a ball, holding myself, wishing I could go back in time to tell Mr. Personality to fuck off with Madame Moirai's offer.

But I couldn't. I'd taken the deal. I signed the nondisclosure paperwork. They owned me. Henri owned me for twenty-four hours.

Tears dribbled down my cheek as I gulped back wild sobs, determined to stuff it down into a deep, black place. Henri leaned over me, his hand lightly caressing my shivering skin. "We shall have so much fun together, you and I, sweet Nicole. You are my most promising purchase to date. I will loathe returning you." He rose and strode away, naked to bark over his shoulder before leaving the room, "Bathe yourself. I will return in an hour."

And then he left, locking the door behind him.

10

I couldn't stay here. Wiping my tears with a savage motion across my face, I scrambled from the bed, going to the window but it was sealed shut. I searched for something in the room to force the window open but there was nothing sharp enough to do the trick.

But as I peered out the window, I realized with a sinking heart, even if I managed to open the window, the drop to the ground would either break my legs or kill me.

I went through the room, frantically looking for something that might help me escape from this prison but it was empty of anything useful.

I found drawers of sex toys and assorted lube that

made me shudder and a closet full of chains, whips, and belts that scared me more than before.

Would Henri beat me? It was within his "right" to do so, according to him. As long as I was returned alive, anything was fair game.

I scurried to the bathroom to check if there was anything I could use as a weapon. Again, disappointed. Unless I wanted to throw small designer bottles of shampoo and body wash at him, I wasn't going to find anything useful.

I bit back a cry of frustration. I would have to finish this hellish game. I eyed the shower as if it were the enemy. It was big enough for at least four people. Showers, in my experience, weren't a social event. Two large rainfall showerheads were placed at each end with smaller showerheads lining the wall. It was, like everything else in this place, ridiculously beautiful but all I saw was the pure indulgence of someone who had too much money and not enough soul.

I stepped into the shower and closed my eyes as I walked under the spray. Steam rose from the hot water as I made the temperature almost unbearable. I welcomed the pain. Rationally, I knew that no matter how hot the water, I would never wash away what'd happened to me.

I viciously scrubbed at my vagina, desperate to get his DNA off of me. Once my skin was reddened and raw, I sat on the tiled ledge and let the water stream down my body. I let the tears flow in the privacy of the shower so the water would wash away my pain.

How did someone recover from an experience like this? Goddamn it, I'd been so fucking naive to think I could sell a piece of myself and walk away with lingering distaste as the only lasting effect.

I thought of Dylan, Jilly, and Tana — my unlikely partners in this game. I worried about Tana most. I wiped at my nose. Was she okay? Would she survive this ordeal? I had no idea how traumatic it would be. If I was struggling, Tana was probably crumpling in on herself.

Dylan seemed badass but who knew what kind of soft spots a hard exterior hides. I didn't believe in God but I needed to cling to something that gave me some kind of hope. I felt empty inside but that wasn't entirely true either because how could an empty space hurt so much?

My hatred for Henri spiraled outward. He was part of the problem but he wasn't the epicenter. Madame Moirai was the one supplying the product. Henri was just like the rest of the disgusting men rich enough to buy people. Removing him from the equation was small and ineffective.

But what was I thinking? I didn't know shit about Madame Moirai's operation and that was purposeful. Questions weren't answered and we were prevented from knowing anything more than what was necessary to finish the deal. Everyone associated with the auction was bound to Madame Moirai just as we were. When people became so powerful that ordinary rules and laws didn't apply to them, it was possible to do anything.

I didn't feel safe.

I shivered in spite of the steam swirling around me. What were the ramifications of killing a girl in these circles? Powerful men weren't about to disappear over a poor girl no one cared about in the first place.

Each of us came from backgrounds that made it possible to manipulate us into taking deals that no sane person ever would.

Desperation was the necessary ingredient to Madame Moirai's toxic soup and damn, that bitch had known exactly who to target for her dinner party.

So, what was I supposed to do now? I guess I had to play the game a little longer. Leaving this place alive and running away from this experience was most important.

I couldn't do that if I was goading Henri. I had no safety net. As much as I loathed him, I would have to find a way to play nice.

He was simply a weak, deviant man with a God complex. If I played to his ego, I might be able to walk away without too many scars.

I just had to find a way to bite my tongue and smile when I wanted to snarl. I had to play the part of the thankful, naive girl who felt fortunate to have a "kind" buyer. Maybe if I was smart enough, I could trick him into sharing information that I might find useful.

I didn't know what I wanted to do with that information but I would feel more secure if I had something — anything — of value to hold onto as leverage.

Hell, maybe it was all wishful thinking and the idea of leverage was an illusion of false hope but it was all I had to cling to. Without it, I'd start screaming and breaking things, which would sure as fuck end badly for me.

Resolved, I turned off the water and wrapped myself in a large, fluffy, pristine white towel that smelled of lavender and expensive things.

I bypassed all of the lotions and perfumes at my disposal. I didn't want any scent to be associated with this experience. The last thing I needed was my nose to remind me of the horrors of this room when I was at the mall or something.

Assuming I escaped this experience alive.

A robe hung on a cloth hanger. The blood-red silk seemed appropriate. My soul was bleeding. I ripped the robe free and wrapped it around me in defiance. Fuck him, I would get through this and thrive in spite of it.

But stupid tears clung to my eyes because the pain inside was like a knife twisting around in my guts. Exactly *how* would I get through this? How would I thrive when I had a cancerous trauma fucking up an already dysfunctional psyche? I didn't have answers, only determination, which summed up my entire damn life.

Madame Moirai had sniffed out my desperation but she hadn't recognized the flip of that coin. If I could turn that to my advantage somehow, I would.

You didn't grow up with Carla West as your mother without learning a few coping mechanisms — unhealthy as they were.

A fire burned inside my belly that Madame Moirai had inadvertently fed. Maybe it wasn't enough to simply survive this night. I'd never been particularly needled by the need for justice in my life but this felt different.

It felt bigger.

We four weren't the first girls to be auctioned off. How many girls had she ruined with her little game? How many souls had she eaten in her pursuit of greed?

The only way to find answers was to insert myself fully into the role I was picked to play.

As much as my stomach turned, I would welcome Henri's touch when he returned. As much as I wanted to stab him in the heart, I would play the part of the contrite and docile slave girl because his monstrous ego was as bloated as his wallet.

I stared into the mirror, seeing someone different. In shitty situations, people could either rise or fall. Carla had chosen to fall. Her weakness dragged her down to wallow in the muck of her own making. I swore I'd be different. I mistakenly thought taking Madame Moirai's deal was smarter than anything Carla had done but it wasn't.

Sucking a dick was sucking a dick. It didn't matter if you were doing it to get some guy to pay for dinner or your future.

Girls had been selling themselves for ages.

Carla had sold her dignity a long time ago and any sense of integrity she might've had was stomped into a puddle of mush way before I came along.

So, I'd sold myself for a bigger payday but here I was, feeling like a bitter whore who'd been cheated her payday and regretting the choice to take the job.

I should've paid better attention to the red flags, much less the fine print.

"Toughen up," I told myself, the hard look in my eyes in direct contrast with the uncontrollable shake in my body. "You will not let this destroy you."

I stared until my body slowly stopped trembling. The girl staring back at me was a million miles away from the smart ass girl who thought she knew more about life than she did. She was also a different person than the girl who gabbed with her bestie about stupid shit that really didn't mean anything in the real world.

Lora was going onto college without a blemish on her soul. I envied her soft childhood, her great parents and overall, wonderful life.

It wasn't about all the birthday cakes, Christmas presents and school lunches my mom conveniently forgot in her single-minded pursuit of a man to help pay the bills — it was about the misery of abject poverty that twisted people into monsters or ground them into dust.

Poverty was a pervasive black mold that invaded and destroyed everything it touched.

Lora would never have to sell herself to be free of the void sucking at her feet, threatening to drag her down into the pits of hell like so many unfortunate people just like me.

She had her family to turn to if she ever fell. I only had myself.

In this moment, for one shame-filled heartbeat, I hated Lora for having everything I'd ever wanted in this life.

I hated that I was the one shivering in a stranger's bathroom, clutching a thin silk to my skin, awaiting my next act of degradation for someone else's entertainment.

It wasn't her fault but was it my fault that fate had put me in Carla's womb instead of that of a decent person?

Fuck, it was an endless pity party if you started down that road, which normally I avoided.

But, forgive me this moment of weepy sadness for myself because, fuck man, this was some terrible shit to navigate for a girl who just wanted a chance to get out from beneath the collapsing shitpile that was her life.

I drew a halting breath, tensing as I heard the lock engaged on the bedroom door. He was back.

I clenched my palms into a tight fist, willing myself to get a grip, willing myself to put on a fake smile and pretend like my life depended on it.

Because I didn't have proof but my gut told me that it did.

I was a survivor. I goddamn better start acting like one.

I opened the door, steam escaping the enclosed space like mist from a sauna to caress my exposed skin.

Henri's eyes lit up with unabashed appreciation, pleased I'd followed his instruction. The smile of the benevolent billionaire had returned as if all was forgiven. "Come, Nicole," he invited, reaching for me. I allowed him to slowly twirl me as he delighted in his shiny, clean toy. The drag of his gaze like fingers across my body, felt intrusive and wicked. "You are exquisite," he murmured, sliding the robe from my shoulders as it pooled at my feet. He met my gaze. "What shall we do now, little bird?"

Assuming pecking your eyes out isn't an option..."Whatever you want," I answered dutifully, settling into the role, pretending to be someone I wasn't. "I'm yours for the night."

"Indeed you are," he agreed, dipping to press his lips against my skin, his tongue darting to taste my collarbone, to nibble on my neck. "Indeed, you are."

I closed my eyes and imagined him dead.

For the first time since starting this journey, a smile found me.

Whatever it took to get through this night...I would do.

11

"I confess, I enjoy this sweeter version of you," Henri said, his satisfied tone grating on my nerves. He was so stupid he couldn't see that I was lying through my teeth and that I loathed everything about him. "You are a smart girl. You've realized with the right attitude much is possible."

I smiled but remained silent. In my experience silence provoked more confessions than questions. People — particularly self-centered narcissists — often couldn't wait to tell you what to think or feel based on their opinion. Henri was turning out to be no different.

"As I said, you are different than most girls from the auction. I like that about you." He leaned forward to murmur, "but what I like most is knowing that you'll always remember that I was first between your legs."

It was a fact I wanted to erase from my memory. "Thank you for being gentle," I lied, pretending to blush. "You were very kind even when I was difficult."

He was feeling generous. Henri chuckled and tweaked my nipple as if it were his right to do so. "All is forgiven," he said. "A show of spirit is good. Fucking a doormat isn't enjoyable."

"I can only imagine," I said.

"Oh, some are dreadfully dull," he shared as if we were true lovers and not victim and rapist. "That's when you have to be creative to liven things up but that wasn't necessary with you. Not that I'd dream of marring that lovely skin. Such a tragedy that would be."

I thought of the closet full of whips and chains he had hidden from view and I smothered a shudder. I had a pretty good idea of how Henri "livened" things up. "

Clearly, Henri liked playing the part of the kinky billionaire with his room full of sexual surprises but I'd happily avoid playing his captive whipping girl for his sick entertainment. Something told me in his world, there was no such thing as a "safe" word.

I deliberately steered the conversation. "This whole arrangement is wild to me," I said, playing the naive child for his benefit. "I mean, for one, it's so crazy that I was picked for this honor but I have no idea how she knew I'd be a good fit. Do you know Madame Moirai? How did you get involved with the auction?"

He bopped me lightly on the nose, something I immediately hated but hid my desire to punch him in the face. "So many questions. I love your lively mind. However, we must remember that too much curiosity can put one such as you in dire circumstances. I wouldn't want anything to happen to you, little bird."

"I'm sorry, I'm just so curious," I said, ducking my gaze. "Forgive me."

"Of course," he said, pulling me into the cove of his arms. I forced myself to relax, swallowing the bile in my throat. "I have a confession, little bird. You make me feel things I haven't felt in a long time. I like this game."

"What game?" I asked.

He rolled me to my back so he could stare down at me with a knowing gaze. "The game where you pretend to be malleable and demure," Henri answered, his gaze narrowing. "I've seen the hatred flash in your eyes and yet you play the softened dove. You amuse me. You are unpredictable. I like it," he decided.

He'd called me out. Maybe he wasn't as stupid as I thought. Or I wasn't as good at hiding my true feelings. Either way, I was found out. I lost the timidity in my tone as I stared up at him. "So what now?" I asked, dropping the useless act. "Are you hoping to *liven* things up by beating me with your assortment of whips and chains?"

"And brutalize that exquisite skin?" he retorted, shaking his head. "No, even I couldn't do something so cruel." He smiled, adding, "At least, not to you." I knew with a certainty that Henri had likely hurt someone else in this room. He was playing a part. In this particular game, he'd decided to play the role of the generous lord, only acting out in cruelty when he deemed it necessary to teach a lesson. *Such as now.* He cupped my breasts, filling his palms as he squeezed almost painfully. "Little bird, you have no true understanding of how lucky you are. Aside from your perfect body, your stubborn little mind fascinates me. Even knowing that you are helpless to stop me from doing anything I please to your body, you still snap and spit your venom. Where do you get such blind courage?"

He was genuinely curious, as if I were a zoo animal on exhibit. I swallowed, answering, "Because I might be poor but I'm not stupid. People have been underestimating me my entire life. I'm a survivor because I've had to be."

"Yes, your drunken mother," he surmised, chuckling at my open shock. He released my breasts to roll to his back with a sigh. "First rule of business, my darling, always know what you're purchasing ahead of time."

My skin crawled. Had Madame Moirai put together a dossier of each of her girls? Like a fucking menu for rich perverts? *Here's a girl with a shitty mother and a chip on her shoulder but a great set of tits and the round bubble butt of a 12-year-old boy. Bidding starts at fifty thousand!* "What else do you know about me?" I asked, barely able to keep the tremble of contempt from my voice.

"I know that you have a nice, tight pussy," he said, rolling me on top of him. "And I know that I find you delectable. Isn't that enough?"

No. "Put yourself in my position."

He found that humorous. "I cannot."

"Try."

A flash of annoyance crossed his expression. "And why would I do that?"

"Have you ever heard of a thing called empathy?"

"Useless in my experience," he answered, his hands anchoring on my hips. "Enough of this talk. I want to feel you all around me."

That was my warning. Either I could submit or he could rape me again, possibly hurting me in the process.

Survival was a double-edged sword. Sometimes you fought so hard to live that you overlooked the reality that living with the consequences could end up being unbearable.

But at this moment, I chose survival. I clung to the determination that he would not break me, no matter what I had to endure.

He knew the moment the gate swung shut on my resistance and the fingers digging into my hips gentled. "Yes, little bird, let me show you how loving I can be," he crooned to me. "I will give you such pleasure that you forget all your complaints. I can make this a dream between you and I."

You're my fucking nightmare, you overindulged piece of European trash. I graced him with a smile that bordered on cocky as I said, "We'll see..." and he chuckled with approval, assuming he'd won.

But he'd never win. He could have my body but

he'd never have my soul or my mind. The Buddhists believed that the body was just a temporary housing for the soul, a vessel for the ongoing journey to enlightenment. I didn't know if I believed in the concept but I was willing to cling to the idea that I was not only the sum of my parts, that I was more than a girl whose body was being violated for someone else's pleasure.

I was more than a collection of cells clumped together. More than the price tag Madame Moirai had placed on my head.

And so much more than Carla West had ever believed I was.

The thing was, being able to disassociate myself from the act being done to me, was my saving grace — the thing that kept me sane — but I knew that someday that bill would come due.

Someday I'd have to deal with the trauma happening to me but I had to live to see that day first.

My gut told me that girls didn't escape Madame Moirai. That some girls never returned home. I refused to be one of those lost girls. I could only pray that each of us returned to the mansion in one piece.

After what felt like an eternity, Henri finished and I was permitted to clean myself in the bathroom. When I returned, food had magically appeared and he looked like a king ready to be hand-fed grapes by my hand. It would take Herculean strength not to choke him with a breadstick.

I wrapped the robe around me as he patted the bed beside him. "Come, little bird, we must eat. You need your strength." I was starving. I gratefully shoved a few pieces of hard cheese in my mouth until he admonished, "Slowly, we mustn't eat like an animal or we shall be treated like one, yes?" I swallowed my bite and nodded, wary at what that would mean. My next bite I was careful to eat more conservatively, gaining his approval. "I've decided to answer one question to sate your curious little mind. I grant you permission to ask whatever you like but be mindful of your question for I will only answer one."

This game was nauseating. One question. He doled out information like a miserly old toad and he enjoyed watching me dangle. The first question that burned in my head was one he likely wouldn't answer, in spite of his promise. I had to ask him something that would seem innocent enough. He was more likely to divulge information that tickled his ego. I placed a grape in my mouth and chewed with great thought before asking, "What is your real name?"

He paused, considering my request. I reminded him playfully, "You promised me one answer. It would mean a lot to me to know who I gave my virginity to."

His gaze hardened. "You gave me nothing, child. I took what I paid for," he corrected me. I nodded, chastised. He chose to forgive me, leaning back with his hands behind his head, his long, lean body stretched out on the bed. I could tell he didn't want to share that information but he must've anticipated that I would ask something of substance, which he found alluring. If anyone was playing a dangerous game, it was Henri.

Unless he knew he had nothing to truly lose because Madame Moirai would ensure my silence — one way or another.

"If you don't want to tell me..."

"Henri Benoit," he finally shared. "Have you heard of my family?" The arrogance in his tone gave me great pleasure when I shook my head with a blank stare. My ignorance dampened his swagger as he said, "Perhaps it isn't your fault. Americans are notoriously poorly educated. My family descends from French nobility."

Was I supposed to be impressed? A pervert was a pervert no matter how you dressed it up to be something it wasn't. My gran used to say you could put a dress on a pig but it didn't make it a princess.

"How lucky you must be," I murmured, hoping that was the right response to keep him talking. "I thought you might be French by your accent but I wasn't sure."

"Indeed. Business brings me to the states quite often but my home is far from here."

"So this isn't your house?" I dared to ask.

"No more questions," he said, rising to go to the dreaded closet of horrors. I swallowed, waiting to find what fresh hell he was going to inflict on me. The curve of his lips worried me as he said, "Take off your robe and come to me, little bird."

I knew whatever was going to happen next would probably live with me for an eternity.

I would endure, I told myself, fighting off frightened tears. I would endure.

And then I would find a way to make that motherfucker pay.

Somehow. Someway.

12

Henri didn't say goodbye and I was glad. I wasn't sure how much longer I could stomach his presence and I knew I was still alive only by his grace, which could be rescinded at his whim with his capricious nature.

As the sun rose, a modest, plain pajama set was delivered to the room with the instructions to dress and be ready for transport in fifteen minutes. I never felt such a wave of gratitude to be leaving this room in my life. I never wanted to see burgundy brocade curtains ever again.

I rose gingerly, every inch of my body reacting in pain as I took my time to dress, wincing as fresh aches and dull agony reminded me how much pleasure Henri had taken in abusing me in his final act.

In spite of his promise that he would be gentle and that he loathed the idea of marking my skin, apparently, he'd changed his mind, proving that his kindness balanced precariously on the edge of his capricious nature.

The memory threatened to send me to my knees but I pushed it away, determined to get away from this place and from him.

There was a reservation in hell for people like Henri Benoit and anyone like him. I hoped he died a thousand different ways when it was his turn to answer for his sins. If that's even a thing that happened. Like I said, I wasn't really into religion and I wasn't entirely sure that God existed but I was willing to hope that if there was a God, there was a devil, too because someone had to make bad people pay.

I started to shake. My fingers struggled with the tiny, pearled buttons but I finally managed to be fully dressed by the time I was shuffled off blindfolded into the awaiting Towncar.

No one spoke to me. I was nothing more than a lump of cargo to them and their job was simple: return the merchandise to the warehouse with no questions asked or answered.

Once in the car, I ripped the blindfold off and

threw it on the floor, whirling to peer out the windows but just as before, the black-out windows blotted out where I was going and where I'd been.

I listened to the sound of the tires on the road. I listened for anything that might give away my location but it was silent, devoid of markers like other cars, city life or even planes overhead, which meant, I was somewhere in the country, away from prying eyes and far from anyone who might rescue me.

The trip was long, at least an hour. When the car rolled to a stop, I hastily grabbed the blindfold and returned it to my eyes, only this time, I left it a little loose so I could see from the bottom at least.

I was jerked from the seat and pushed forward, a far cry from the restrained courtesy when I first arrived, and after climbing the stairs, sent almost tumbling into a room. I pulled the blindfold free but not before the door closed and locked behind me.

This was a different room than before. Instead of four beds, there was only one with a small desk and chair. It was simply furnished, nothing spoke of luxury or wealth. If anything, it looked like an upscale prison cell for minimum security prisoners. Or maybe a group home.

The bedding was plain cotton and the bathroom adjoining was nothing like the sumptuous extravaganza from before. A toilet, a small, functional shower, a few folded towels and a set of hotel toiletries were all that could be found in the room. No more fancy perfumes and lotions. No huge Jacuzzi tub with bath bombs or essential oils. A sense of foreboding lodged itself in my gut as the message we no longer held any value was hammered home.

I went to the door and tried to open it. As before, locked. I started to pace the small room. Panic and claustrophobia setting in at once. I tried to calm my breathing but my heart was racing. I banged on the door, yelling, "I want to talk to Olivia!" but when nothing but silence answered me, I gave the door a solid kick, bruising my toe but accomplishing little else.

I sat on the edge on the bed, waiting, because it was all I could do. Silence was my enemy. The quiet only gave my mind permission to replay my time with Henri and I wanted to puke.

I could still smell him on my skin. I could taste him in my mouth. The bruising of his fingers lingered on my flesh.

I could feel the bile rising in my throat as I tried to keep it down. I lost the battle and ran for the toilet, unloading the small bites of food I'd managed to get down last night when Henri was feeling generous. I heaved until nothing remained and I started to dry heave until I thought I might vomit a kidney.

Finished, I wiped at my mouth and flushed before dropping to the cold tile floor. I wanted to shower but I didn't have the strength to stand just yet. Not enough food, too much exertion and emotional trauma collided to steal the strength from my legs.

I didn't know how long I sat crumpled on that floor, staring at the wall, seeing nothing. Finally, I unfurled myself from a curled position and crawled to the shower. I stripped and stood beneath the spray, grateful for the simple pleasure of hot water sluicing over my body, washing away the pain but not the memory.

Tears I didn't want to cry, crowded my sinuses. My chest burned with the need to scream. I stuffed it all down but it kept rising to choke the air from my lungs. I pressed my forehead against the cool ceramic tiles, bracing myself with my hands, water running down my back.

This too shall pass.

I was alive, that's what mattered — and I intended to stay that way.

They would not destroy me. I wouldn't give them

that power. If my own mother couldn't kill my spirit, some overprivileged dickwad wouldn't either. I was stronger than anything they could throw at me. I'd show them that they haven't won but I could only do that if I wasn't folding in on myself, wanting to die.

When I felt I could successfully leave the shower without collapsing, I toweled off and redressed in the pajamas I was in before.

With nothing but my thoughts to keep me company, I curled up on the bed and fell fast asleep, thankful my dreams were nothing but a black void of exhaustion.

I woke hours later just in time for Olivia to enter with a tray of food and a sunny smile as if I wasn't a prisoner in this place.

She set the tray down and came to join me, sitting in the chair opposite the bed. "How are you feeling?" she asked as if that weren't an absurd question.

I wasn't in the mood for small talk. "Where's everybody else?" I demanded to know. "Why aren't we all in the same room as before?"

Olivia smiled. "You should eat. You're probably exhausted."

"Where are Jilly, Dylan, and Tana?" I asked,

stubbornly refusing to be deflected. "What's going on? This doesn't feel right."

"You have a suspicious mind," Olivia said, that stupid smile never slipping, as if she were indulging my silly questions. "Everyone is fine. Resting, same as you. It's customary for the girls to be alone after their time with the buyers so they might enjoy some peace and quiet. I would imagine you've earned it."

Fuck her for knowing what we'd been through and that we'd probably welcome solitude. I hated to admit that made a certain level of sense. Was I being paranoid? Was the deal truly everything it seemed to be and now that the hard part was over, I was about to get a big, fat check? "What happens now?" I asked, still not trusting Olivia or anything associated with Madame Moirai.

"You will be seen by a physician, given a few days of rest and then, depending on your circumstances, either sent home or elevated."

"Elevated? What the fuck does that mean?" I asked. "I don't understand. What are you talking about? I just want to be paid and then I want the fuck out of here."

"Of course. Please, enjoy some food and I'll be back in the morning to discuss your options."

"I want to see the girls," I persisted, needing to know that they were okay, too. "Especially Tana."

Olivia's expression changed for only a second as she asked in confusion, "Why?"

"Because she was having a hard time before the auction and I want to make sure she's okay."

"She's fine," Olivia assured me but the woman had the warmth of a snake. "Now, is there anything else you require for the night? Books, perhaps?"

"I told you what I wanted. To see the girls."

"Right. That's not going to happen," she answered, rising. "They need their rest, just as you need yours. I'm sorry, Madame Moirai is quite strict in that regard. All protocols must be followed as I'm sure you remember from your contract."

No, I didn't remember shit about this part in the contract but honestly, I didn't think anything in that damn document made any fucking sense aside from the money that was supposed to land in my account. Speaking of, "When do I get paid?" I asked as Olivia headed for the door.

"All in due time," she answered without looking at me. "Goodnight."

The door closed and, as always, locked from the outside. "Fuck," I muttered, rising as I went to survey the food situation. Chicken, mashed potatoes and green beans. Not the most inventive of meals but it smelled edible. Now that Henri wasn't here to chastise my table manners, I shoved the food in my mouth with the ravenous force worthy of my grumbling stomach.

Finished, I let out a loud belch in defiance of Olivia's prissy, practiced civility and crawled back into the bed with a full belly. I didn't think I would fall asleep again so quickly but exhaustion had a way of sapping your energy before you realized you were spent.

But something was scratching at the back of my brain.

Paranoia had its place. My gut was telling me that something was off. Something that Olivia wasn't sharing. What the hell did "elevate" mean? Why was she so sketchy about explaining? And why the fuck was I locked in the room like an animal? I felt like a prisoner, which had only marginally made sense before the auction — maybe Madame Moirai wanted to make sure no one reneged on their contract — but now that it was all done, what was the point of locking us in?

And why did a physician need to see us? I didn't want another fucking shot. And if anyone comes near me with another enema I'd start swinging fists.

That was a promise.

It's almost over, I told myself as I drifted to sleep. Almost.

My last thoughts were of Tana. I didn't care what Oliva said, I wouldn't rest easy until I saw Tana with my own two eyes.

13

As Olivia said, bright and early, I was brought from my room and taken to another room that was outfitted like an exam room in a doctor's office. Everything was cut and dry, the doctor barely made eye contact, just treated me like a prized heifer who was getting a final check before the sale was finalized.

"Why are you doing this?" I asked.

"Do you have any sharp pains in your stomach or pelvic region?" he asked, ignoring my question.

"Yeah, I feel like I've been beaten and fucked up the ass, which I was. You mean, pain like that?" I shot back, watching for his reaction but there was none. Jesus, had the man no heart? "Do you even care?"

"I'm going to do a pelvic exam. Scoot down, please."

I stared in disbelief. "I just want to go home. I'm being held like a fucking prisoner. Whatever happened to your doctor oath? Harm none, or something like that? Can you honestly say I haven't been harmed? What you're doing is disgusting, helping these people hurt girls. Have you no shame?"

"Scoot down, please." The hard edge to his tone made me shiver. I realized no help would come from him. Just like everyone else in this God-forsaken place, he had no empathy because we weren't looked at as people. I slowly inched my way down, my legs opening for the intrusive exam. The doctor made quick work of swabbing my insides and doing a cursory check, then pulling his gloves with a snap, he announced, "All good. You may sit up now."

I guess I passed the test. No lasting damage to my body, just my mind but who cared about that, right?

"Have you examined the other girls, yet?" I asked. Again, silence. I tried again. "Are you not allowed to talk or something? Like, does Madame Moirai have you by the short hairs or something? Is she blackmailing you to be her private doctor? You know what's happening isn't right but you're doing it anyway. Either you're a piece of shit or you're being pressed into service, just like the rest of us. So... which is it?"

The doctor regarded me with irritation, stating, "You talk entirely too much."

"Consequence of not being dumb as fuck, I guess."

"You would do well to watch what you say."

Was that advice or a threat? Maybe it was both. "Why are we locked in our rooms? The auction is over. Our part is done. We should be free to leave. What's happening to us now?"

"Once you're determined to be in good health, you're free to go," he answered with a bland smile that I didn't trust at all. I read once that dogs were a good judge of character. I didn't need a dog to sniff out that this guy was rotten.

"Yeah? I think you're lying," I called him out. "I think we're never leaving this awful place, which is why we're locked in our rooms." He pulled a large syringe and I immediately shrank away. "What the fuck is that for?"

"Precautionary measure. Turn on your side, please."

"Precautionary measure against what?"

He met my gaze without blinking, answering flatly, "STDs."

"But I was checked before the auction and I was clean."

The heavy silence told me that I may have been clean but that's not to say all the buyers were. I wanted to scream at him but rolled to my side so he could jab that horse needle in my butt cheek. Tears sprang to my eyes as the pain of whatever was in that fucking needle made me want to cry out but I bit back the urge.

"All done," he announced. "You may get dressed. The site will be sore for a few days but you should be clear of anything going forward. Someone will bring you back to your room in a few moments."

And then he left. I tore the paper gown from my body and quickly dressed, wincing as the pain from the shot radiated through my muscles.

I guess I should be thankful for the after-care? Maybe. I still didn't trust them as far as I could throw them. Something felt off.

I tried the door but like the rest, it was locked from the outside.

I jumped back as the door opened and a guard grabbed me by the arm to drag me back to my room. I didn't see a gun but I sensed that he was packing.

The cruel bite of his fingers into my arm told me everything I needed to know.

Madame Moirai filled her payroll with people who were monsters.

"How do you sleep at night?" I muttered to the guard.

"Like a baby," he surprised me with an answer. "You signed up for this. Stop bitching."

My cheeks flared with heat as shame rolled over me. "You have no idea what I was trying to escape so don't fucking judge me."

"I could give two shits about your life, you stupid little cunt. You're getting paid so shut the fuck up and do as you're told."

"I haven't been paid yet," I shot back, yanking on my arm but his grip was like iron. Did Madame Moirai hire disgraced Marines to patrol her property? Fuck it, I probably wasn't getting out alive so might as well push my luck a little further. I added with a glare, "And I have a feeling I'm not *ever* going to get paid so fuck you with your judgment because if I'm a piece of shit, so are you!"

He jerked me around and shoved me against the wall, my head hitting with a hard thump. His fingers curled around my throat, anchoring me painfully as I tried to push him away. He leaned in, his breath smelling like curly fries and cigarette smoke. "You should watch your mouth, *whore*," he said. "You think you're hot shit because some asshole paid to fuck you? Well, you're not. You're nothing. So be thankful that you're getting a nice bed, decent food, and medical care because a girl like you ain't worth shit. Get that through your thick skull and stop making trouble or else you're going to wish you'd taken my advice when you're gagging on a dirty cock in a back alley somewhere for a twenty-dollar bill. You hear me?"

Tears brimmed in my eyes as fear clamped down around me but I met his gaze and managed to croak, "Fuck. You," while smiling at his rage.

Murder flashed in his eyes. What the fuck was wrong with me that I had zero common sense? Why was I goading this asshole into hurting me? I knew the answer. I'd rather die than let some dick like him know that I was scared. "Go ahead," I taunted. "Do your worst but something tells me if you put your hands on me, you'll have to answer to Madame Moirai for marking up her merchandise. You want to chance pissing her off?" I must've said something that rang with truth. His grip loosened and he let go. I didn't hide the victory in my tone as I sneered in contempt, "That's what I thought" but I didn't have long to gloat. He grabbed me by my hair and threw me into the room, slamming the door behind me.

I fell to the plush carpet, scuffing my palms with rug burn but I laughed maniacally as I rolled to my back. Everyone was so afraid of Madame Moirai they weren't willing to do shit to help us. We were so screwed. I flopped to my side and hugged my knees to my chest, curling in a ball. My ass cheek burned as if the doctor had lodged a fiery hot ember beneath my skin. What was going to happen to us? The contract said five days but I didn't believe we would walk away from this contract. Somehow she'd find a way to keep us and I didn't know how we'd get free.

We were surrounded by gun-packing guards with hearts of stone. Every single person we'd come into contact with were lock-stock-and-barrel with Madame Moirai. Either she paid really well for their silence or she had something on them to force their cooperation.

Either way, it came out bad for us because they weren't going to lift a fucking finger to help.

I unfurled myself and rose to my feet, rubbing at my neck where that brute had assaulted me. My skin was reddened but was otherwise fine.

I paced the small room, feeling the sticky fingers of claustrophobia clawing at my throat as panic threatened. *Get a grip! You won't survive if you freak out! Think smart.* Nodding in response to my internal pep talk, I went to the bathroom and splashed some water on my face, taking a minute to calm my racing heart. Nothing was impossible. There were always ways around a problem. I eyed the door. It was locked from the outside but it wasn't a deadbolt. It was a simple lock with weaknesses. Underestimating someone's determination to succeed was the first mistake most people made. Madame Moirai purposefully went after girls who she perceived as vulnerable and vulnerable people tended to take fewer chances because they were scared of retribution.

Except me.

I had a stubborn streak a mile long jammed into my spine. Carla had tried to beat it out of me but she finally gave up because, in the end, I was stronger than she was — or ever would be.

So, these assholes weren't going to break me, either.

With the right tools, I could jimmy the lock.

I returned to the bedroom with a critical eye. I checked under the bed, combed through the carpet, looked under every surface, every nook and cranny of the room, including the bathroom.

Just as I was about to give up, I found a bobby pin hiding in the seam where the carpet met the wall that must've been missed in a previous clean up. I smiled. If one was missed, there was likely more. I crawled along the seam of the carpet, my fingers digging and feeling for anything that felt like it didn't belong. At the furthest edge of the room, I found another bobby pin, flung and forgotten, nearly lost in the minute crack.

All I needed were two.

Hiding the pins beneath my pillow, I formulated a plan after the house went dark.

When Olivia returned with my dinner, I was ready to play the part she wanted to see.

Olivia regarded me with wary speculation as she set my dinner tray down. "You seem more agreeable this evening. How are you feeling?"

"Sore from the shot but after I thought about it, I realized it was smart," I said, sniffing at the air, "Wow, smells good. What's for dinner?"

"Meatloaf."

"I love meatloaf," I lied with a smile. "Always reminds me of my grandmother."

"Your grandmother...I thought the only family you had was your mother."

I affected a sad expression, clarifying, "She died when I was six."

Satisfied, Olivia nodded. "And from what I understand you and your mother have a strained relationship?"

Strained. That was a mild word to describe the outright animosity between myself and my mother. I knew why Olivia was asking and it sent a chill down my back. I decided to play loose with the truth. "Well, I mean, we're not the closest but she *is* my mom. I'm sure if I disappeared she'd be really upset and call the cops," I finished with a short smile.

Olivia's equally short, cold smile told me my answer hadn't pleased her. *Good. Choke on it, you twisted bitch.* Olivia clasped her hands in front of her, replying, "Of course, as any good mother should." She paused a minute before adding with a chiding expression, "However, would you really say Carla West was a good mother?"

No, Carla was a shit mother but I wasn't going to let Olivia have the satisfaction of knowing she was right. It was a silly test of wills but I was determined to win. I exhaled with a shrug, answering, "She did the best that she could. I know she loves me. That's good enough for me."

"Indeed." Olivia turned to leave but I stopped her with a question.

"My five days will be up soon. When will I be leaving?"

"Details are being prepared," Olivia said. "Patience is a virtue."

"Patience has never been my thing," I admitted. "I'm ready to sleep in my own bed, go back to school, you know, normal kid stuff. College applications to fill out with my best friend, that kinda thing. Now that I'll have money in the bank, I don't have to worry about applying for student loans."

Olivia's smile never faltered and she didn't respond. She closed the door behind her, locking it tight.

I dropped the fake smile and stared hard enough to burn a hole through the door, wishing I had a laser in my hand to sear that awful smug, prissy expression clean off Olivia's face.

I could only imagine what went through Olivia's head as I prattled on about college when she knew Madame Moirai owned my future. Well, fuck that. Madame Moirai wasn't going to get another piece of me and I'd do anything to make sure of that.

One way or another, I was getting out of this place.

14

Waiting for the house to quiet under the cover of night was the longest wait of my life. It was near one in the morning when I finally felt it was safe enough to try and pick the lock.

I fished the bobby pins from beneath my pillow and went to work. It took about fifteen minutes of frustrating failures to finally hear the tumblers flick into place, disengaging the lock.

I wiped at the sweat beading my forehead, my heartbeat racing like a wild thing. I drew a few deep breaths and then quietly and carefully opened the door a sliver to peer out. Darkened hallways were blessedly empty, which meant the guards — especially the one who already wanted to beat me to a pulp — were elsewhere.

I strained to pick up any sound that might give away someone walking around.

My ears picked up nothing but the ordinary sounds of deep night surrounding a sleeping house.

In their arrogance, they must've thought we were docile little pigeons in our cages, afraid to push against a locked door. I was more than happy to take advantage of their stupidity.

The plush carpet pad beneath my feet cushioned my steps as I made my way down the hallway, careful to remain in the shadows, just in case.

The long hall was punctuated by closed doors. I padded silently to the first door and saw that it wasn't locked. No sense in wasting time looking there as they wouldn't keep any of us in an unlocked room.

I tried the next door and saw that is was locked. I slowly turned the lock so that it didn't make a sound. I slipped quietly inside and closed the door, my heart pounding. My eyes adjusted to the dark and I saw a lump in the bed. The room was the same as mine, utilitarian and functional but nothing that screamed luxury. I tiptoed over to the bed and knelt beside the sleeping figure.

The figure shifted in the bed with a small moan. My heart leaped. Relief washed over me as I sensed that it was Dylan. I gently covered her mouth so she didn't scream, whispering, "Dylan, it's me, Nicole. Don't make a sound."

The moonlight streaming in from the window cast a bluish-grey light on the room. Dylan sat up with difficulty, as if she were in pain, and peered at me in confusion. "Nicole?" she croaked, her voice clogged with sleep. "What are you doing here?"

I was so happy to see her, I didn't mind that it was Dylan I found first when I'd been hoping to find Tana. "I snuck out of my room," I explained in a hushed tone. "I had to see if anyone else was here like me. Olivia wouldn't give me any answers no matter how many times I asked. They've got us locked in prison cells. Something feels off. Are you okay?"

Dylan rubbed at her eyes, becoming more fully awake. She winced as she moved to a better position. "Yeah, I guess. Sore. You?"

"I'll live," I answered. "Has Olivia said anything to you about when you get to leave? Our five days is almost up."

"No. I haven't seen Olivia. A guard shoves a platter of cold oatmeal at me and then locks the door again."

"Oatmeal?" I repeated in confusion. "Why?"

"How the fuck should I know? Maybe because they don't want to spend any more money on us and that includes decent food. I fucking hate oatmeal but I've choked it down because I'm so hungry."

"Did you get a check-up from the doctor and an STD shot?"

"No, I was just stuck in this room even though I'm beaten to shit. I swear I think that fucker broke a few toes and definitely a finger but they haven't sent a doctor to check me out. Why?"

I felt a sense of foreboding as I shared, "A doctor looked me over and gave me an STD shot today. I've also been getting better food. Not four-star restaurant but chicken and mashed potatoes, that kind of stuff."

"What the fuck?" Dylan exclaimed until I shushed her to keep her voice down. Dylan glared as if somehow it was my fault. "Why? What makes you so special?"

"I don't know," I answered truthfully "but something tells me being *special* in this place isn't necessarily a good thing."

She conceded my point grudgingly. "I think you're right. What if they're planning to keep you here for other clients?"

The idea made my blood run cold. I'd die first

before I let that happen. "No fucking way. I'll chew my way out of here if I have to."

"I don't know if anyone gets out of here. We're in a prison. The only thing missing is an ankle bracelet."

"Look, I'm going to see if I can find the other girls and then we're going to get the fuck out of this hell-hole, got it?"

With a sudden urgency, she asked, "Did you find anyone besides us on this floor?"

I answered with wary confusion, "No? I mean, yours is the first locked door I opened. Why?"

She exhaled, looking away, saying, "I don't know, I mean if we got roped into this deal, there's probably others, too."

I wasn't leading a revolution. I just wanted to get the three of us out. "Yeah, well, I don't know but it's pretty quiet. It seems like it might just be us."

Dylan swallowed, nodding. "Yeah, probably." She met my gaze to ask, "Why didn't you just run while you had the chance?"

"Because I couldn't leave knowing you guys were still stuck here." That was partially true. The harsh truth was that I probably would've ditched the other girls if Tana had been behind that door. I was a little ashamed but I couldn't lie to myself. For some reason, I couldn't bring myself to leave without Tana. Now that I'd found Dylan, I was committed to finding Jilly, too. "Listen, just act like nothing is different," I instructed. "I don't want Olivia getting the sense that we're up to something. Right now, she's thinking that I've accepted her word that we're going home but I can tell she's lying."

"You think so?"

I nodded. "I can't explain it — call it my gut instinct — but they have no intentions of letting us go much less paying us and I've got a bad feeling about how they get out of paying."

Dylan stared at me. "But we signed a fucking contract," she said.

"I think that was just for appearances. I mean, it was pretty convincing, right?"

"Yeah," Dylan said faintly, processing. "Fuck. It was all a lie."

"Which is why we need to get the fuck out of here."

I paused, my eye-catching the dark bruising on Dylan's face as my eyes further adjusted to the dim light. Dylan caught me staring. "Stop," she said, looking away. "I know I look like shit."

"What happened?" I asked, my voice softening with horror for Dylan. "What did he do?"

Dylan shook her head, a slight catch in her voice as she answered, "I don't want to talk about it."

I hoped they all rotted in hell for what they'd done to us. I swallowed, allowing a moment of silence between us. I understood why Dylan would rather bury the memory than relive it.

I didn't want to talk about my ordeal either. My physical body might not have the same bruises as Dylan but I felt the pain in my soul. "I'm sorry," I murmured, my understanding the only solace I could offer. We might not like each other but we were bonded by our shared trauma. "We're going to get out of here," I promised her.

Dylan looked away but not before I caught the sheen of unshed tears in her eyes. For some reason that brief reveal on Dylan's part gut-punched me harder than I expected but when she said in a choked whisper, "He didn't like questions. He..."

I gently gripped her hand in mine and she gulped back her words as I said softly, "You don't have to tell me. I understand."

She jerked a nod and we let silence absorb our hurt for the moment. I never knew what real monsters roamed the earth hidden behind the protection of finely tailored suits and privileged connections until now. Scary stories were supposed to have vampires and werewolves or some kind of supernatural bad guy but in reality, people were the ultimate villain. The cost of my ignorance was more than I could bear but for the moment, I had to let it go.

The shame, the terror, the rage — I couldn't afford feeling any of that right now. I promised myself a proper freak-out, melt-down when I was free of this horrid place and I could collapse in the privacy of my own space. Not here and definitely not now.

I drew a shaky breath. "Look, we're going to make them all pay. I don't know how but we will. First, we need to find our way out. I need you to keep playing whatever part keeps them comfortable.

"Have you heard anything about Jilly or Tana?"

"Not a word. No one answers any questions around here. Especially the guards. Bunch of dicks with guns. There's one fucker that's a real asshole. Probably has tiny dick syndrome and tries to make up for it by beating up on people weaker than him."

I knew exactly who she was referring to. "Yeah, I think I met him. He tried to choke me out until I reminded him that his boss might not want her property marked up. It worked. Apparently, Madame Moirai's reach is pretty long."

"Great," Dylan quipped. "We're totally fucked."

"No, I don't accept that. She can kiss my ass as I run from this place."

"We don't even know where we are," Dylan said. "It's not like we can call an Uber to get us."

"We have feet. We'll run, crawl, or whatever it takes. Either you want to live or you want to die here, Dylan. You have to make the choice because I'm not dragging dead weight."

I was being serious. I would leave her ass behind if she lagged. I couldn't spend time pulling someone who didn't want to go.

"Calm down, I'm not saying I want to fucking stay," Dylan grumbled, pulling the blankets up a little higher. "I want out just as much as you."

"Good." I rose. "Be ready to bail as soon as I come get you. I'm going to see if I can find Jilly and Tana. Stay safe."

I got to the door and Dylan called out softly, "Hey," and I turned around in question. "Thanks for coming to find me."

I nodded and slipped quietly out into the hall.

I tried a few more doors but found nothing. I knew I couldn't risk being found so I hurried back to my room, locking the door as I closed it with a soft *snick*.

I climbed back into my bed and snuggled down into the blankets, adrenaline pounding in my ears. I was so afraid Olivia was going to burst into my room knowing I'd been out but as the moments ticked by and the house remained as quiet as before, I relaxed and let myself fall asleep.

It seemed I'd pulled off my unscheduled tour of the house.

Tomorrow night, I'd do it again.

15

The next morning, I showered and found a fresh pair of clothes waiting for me, along with Olivia who brought my breakfast tray. I thought of Dylan and her daily meal of oatmeal and I wanted to throw the upgraded meal in Olivia's face but I didn't. Instead, I wrapped the robe around myself a little more tightly and sat on the bed to start eating.

Olivia, wearing her usual practiced smile, waited for me to take a few bites of the scrambled eggs before saying, "I'm glad to see your appetite has flourished. We mustn't let ourselves become malnourished. It's bad for the skin. Drink plenty of water to retain that youthful glow."

Youthful glow? I was a fucking teenager. If my skin didn't glow naturally I had problems. But forgive me, if I thought her advice was total bullshit. I wanted to quip, '*Yeah? Well, you know what else is good for a youthful glow? Not being caged in a locked room for days on end.*' But I kept my mouth occupied with food, which seemed a safer plan.

Olivia pulled a small notebook from her pocket as if to take notes. *This was new*, I noted, chewing slowly. "What's up?" I asked, going straight for the obvious. "What's with the notebook?"

"We like to keep a detailed record of Madame Moirai's girls for our accounting purposes. I hope you don't mind answering a few questions."

Yes, I did mind but that probably wasn't the right answer. I forced a shrug along with a fresh bite of bacon as if I didn't sense that Olivia was fishing for information for a bad purpose. "Shoot," I said, pretending as if I didn't care.

Pleased, Olivia said, "Excellent," preparing to continue. "All right, you're a senior at Carvello High, correct?"

I nodded, throwing in, "Looking forward to graduating now that I have the funds to go to college" just to make her squirm.

As expected, Olivia bypassed my comment and moved on. "Any family history of cancer, disease or mental illness?"

"Seems like that's a question that should've been asked *before* I signed the contract but, no, I don't have any of those things, unless you can count signing up for this gig as totally fucking nuts, which it kinda is." I finished with an angelic smile meant to irritate the prissy cunt. "I guess *you'll* have to figure out how to categorize that decision."

"You have a criminal record," she stated, as if needing me to verify the facts.

I refused to be embarrassed. Instead, I owned it. "Yeah, my mom forced me to shoplift for her because I was a minor and less likely to get any time. She was wrong. I spent a month in juvie for her crime. Life's a bitch, right?" I wiped my mouth, finished, adding, "But now that I'm eighteen, my record should be sealed. How'd you get that info?"

"We're very thorough."

"Probably helps to have someone on the inside, too," I fished but Olivia didn't take the bait.

"No surviving family aside from your mother?"

I held her expectant stare for a long moment before answering with an exaggerated, "Nope."

"Excellent."

I cocked my head in question. "And why is that excellent? I think it's kinda sad. Do *you* have any family? Anyone who might miss you if you suddenly, oh, I don't know, disappeared?"

"We aren't talking about me, we're talking about you," Olivia sidestepped my question neatly. She closed her notebook and tucked it into her pocket once more. That smile I was beginning to hate reappeared. "I have some exciting news to share."

"Oh? We get to go home today?" I guessed with a hopeful expression. "I mean, our five days is just about up so I figured it was around the corner, which is good because I've got plans with my best friend that include some much-needed shopping."

I was prattling nonsense on purpose. I wanted her to feel uncomfortable with whatever she was going to say next. I knew Madame Moirai wasn't planning on letting us go home. Not now, probably not ever but I wanted the bitch's emissary to admit it herself.

She folded her hands in her lap. "You are one lucky young lady. From time to time, Madame Moirai sees something special in an auction girl and decides to offer that girl an 'elevation' from her current status to one with more esteem." Her smile widened as if she were about to announce I'd won the lottery. "And you, Nicole, have caught Madame

Moirai's eye as someone who might be worthy of elevation."

"That sounds like a cult," I said, unimpressed. "Sorry, but I have a strict 'No cult joining' policy in my life. I'd rather just get paid and put this whole situation behind me."

"It's a great honor," Olivia insisted, dropping her smile. "Of the many girls who are chosen for the auction, only a select few get the privilege of elevating."

"Yeah, sounds like a big deal but it's just not for me," I said, but I was curious as to what exactly elevation meant. "For argument's sake...what exactly does it mean to become elevated?"

Oliva's smile returned. Was this woman a robot, programmed to react in certain ways to select keywords? *Yeesh.* She was creepy as fuck. "It would seem that your buyer has taken quite a shine to you. He's interested in pursuing a more long-term relationship with you. Isn't that lovely?"

Lovely? No, Olivia, that's a fucking horror story. "He raped me," I said flatly, unable to pretend I was anything but repulsed by my buyer. "I would never pursue anything more with that fucking monster."

Olivia's expression hardened. "We don't use that

word here. You mustn't spread rumors or lies, Nicole. You and I both know that's not what happened. You were paid for a service that you agreed upon in writing."

"No, actually, I haven't been paid shit yet and even if I had, he still raped me. Does Madame Moirai even care what happens to the girls she sells off to the highest bidder? Or is that just inconsequential noise in the background?"

I was blowing my own plan to play the game but the minute Olivia mentioned Henri, I wanted to puke. I would die before I returned to his care.

"You're being difficult."

"And you're not listening to me."

"Let me speak plainly...you signed a contract for sex. What did you think was going to happen?"

I glared. "Not what he did to me."

She shrugged, saying, "You seem fine to me. Aside from some light bruising, you were otherwise returned in excellent shape. You're acting the spoiled child and it's unattractive. You agreed to the terms," she reminded me.

"No one told me what the fine print truly entailed and you know it. Don't pretend that Madame Moirai's stupid contract was completely transparent with what might happen to us. I sure as hell don't remember signing off on being imprisoned after the deed was done."

"Don't be so dramatic. This is hardly a prison," Olivia said.

"I'm locked in with three hots and a cot. Sounds like prison to me. Except prisoners usually have access to cable television at least."

"Madame Moirai believes television erodes your mental health."

"I believe being raped eroded my mental health more." I paused before adding, "Do you ever have trouble sleeping at night? Just wondering."

Her nostrils flared, her lips compressing. I didn't care that I was stomping on her nerves. The bitch deserved it.

"You seem pretty comfortable passing judgment when you were more than willing to do whatever it took to get the cash," Olivia said with barely contained anger, as if I were being petty and it was her job to point it out. "It's a little bit of the pot calling the kettle black, wouldn't you say?"

"Not even in the slightest," I disagreed hotly. "You people target girls who are desperate but you don't tell them what really happens because if they had any sense they'd run and then where would Madame Moirai get fresh product?" I skewed my gaze at her, narrowing my stare in speculation. "Were *you* elevated? Is that why you're part of this nightmare machine? I can't imagine why anyone would want to be part of this scheme unless they were forced but you seem to enjoy the misery of others so, which is it — forced or willing?"

Color flushed Olivia's cheeks and her eyes flashed with something that resembled human emotion but she shut it down as quickly as it flared. She rose, irritated, "I'm going to give you time to rethink your rash decision as well as your hurtful and damaging words. Henri is one of our best clients and it's a privilege to be asked to be his long-term companion. You're passing up an opportunity of a lifetime. Don't be naive. This is the golden ticket if you're smart enough to see what you're being offered."

"My answer is no." I wasn't going to budge.

Olivia went to the door, her expression pinched. She turned to me before leaving, saying in a clipped tone, "I think a little time to reflect on your choices would be wise. I'll return when you've come to your senses."

The door shut behind her, locking as always.

If that were the case, I'd rot in this room. I wasn't going to change my mind. Not ever.

Now I knew why I was getting preferential treatment. My 'elevated' status meant I needed additional care. Henri wanted me returned to his bed so he could abuse me some more. I was the prized pig, being kept safe and plump in my cage until it was time to deliver me to my master.

I couldn't imagine anything more loathsome than feeling Henri sweating and grunting on top of me again. To feel his fingers on my skin, or taste him in my mouth. I suppressed a shudder. I would gladly and defiantly walk headlong into a raging fire rather than suffer anything Henri would force upon me.

How did someone lose so much of their humanity that they could hurt others like this?

Did they ever lose sleep at night for the things they'd done? *Likely not.*

I thought I'd seen the worst humanity could dish out but now I realized I'd been embarrassingly naive. Humble pie tasted like sour milk, fear, and degradation when Madame Moirai was the baker.

Jesus, who were these people? They were criminals. People with crazy money were plain, straight-up evil. Olivia could shove that notebook up her ass. I wasn't going to change my mind or ever agree to spend another minute with Henri Benoit.

He was the worst kind of evil. On the surface, he

looked disarmingly charming. Good looks and a refined air hid his black heart. I hated him. I hated everything he stood for. I hated myself for being so stupid as to miss that I was being conned.

I should've known Henri wouldn't let me go so easily. He'd already told me that night I was unlike anyone he'd ever had and that most people bored him. Except me. I'd fascinated Henri. How could I have known that Henri's seemingly innocuous compliment would mean my ruin?

I needed to find Jilly and Tana so we could get the hell out of here. Tonight, I wouldn't return to my room until I'd found them both.

Time was running out.

For all of us.

16

Night fell and a platter of oatmeal was delivered to my room. I smirked at the downgrade, obviously a punishment for my bad attitude with Olivia earlier, but I didn't care. She could suck my dick if she thought I gave two shits about her feelings. She could talk to me until she was blue in the face about what an honor it was to be thrown back into the arena with the wolves but I wasn't buying.

I was blowing this popsicle stand as soon as I could make it happen.

I waited patiently for the house to settle and then, same as before, picked the lock with my bobby pins and slipped into the hall unseen.

I clung to the shadows like a ninja, my feet making no sound on the plush carpet. I bypassed

Dylan's room and kept going to the first room I hadn't tried yet. I saw the lock engaged, which gave me hope. I silently turned the lock and snuck inside, closing the door with zero sound.

My eyes adjusted to the darkness and I went to the sleeping form in the bed. I recognized Jilly's pixie haircut. I gently shook her awake. Her eyes flew open with a small gasp but when she saw that it was me, her arms flew around me like I was a guardian angel.

I wasn't a hugger by nature but I sensed that Jilly needed that comfort and held her tight. Jilly released me and I saw tears dribbling down her cheek. She whispered in confusion, "How did you get in here?"

"I picked the lock," I answered. "Let's just say I picked up some skills from my childhood that aren't quite legal."

Jilly nodded. "Are you okay?"

"I'm will be as soon as we get the fuck out of here. What are they feeding you?"

Jilly frowned, answering, "Lukewarm oatmeal. It's like a bowl of glue. I can only eat a few bites before it makes me want to gag. Why?"

"They're feeding me differently."

"What do you mean?"

"Olivia said Madame Moirai sometimes chooses

to elevate certain girls. They're treated better than the rest. I guess I was chosen."

"Chosen for what? What does it mean to be elevated?"

"In my case, it means my buyer wants another round for an indeterminate amount of time."

Even in the dim light, I could see the color drain from Jilly's face as she looked at me with ghostly fear. "Oh my God, what are you going to do?"

"Isn't it obvious? I'm bailing on this shit show."

"But what about the money? If you bail, you won't get paid."

I grasped Jilly's hand before delivering the awful truth, "None of us are getting paid. It's all a fucking lie. Think about it, why do you think they have you locked in a room, feeding you nothing but garbage? When we first got here, they treated us like we were worth something at least. Now? We're just used goods. Something bad is about to happen to all of us. I should've known this was too good to be true and now I see how she pulls off this scam."

Jilly's eyes watered. "You mean we went through this for nothing? How do you know? Are you sure? I mean, what if you're wrong?"

I could feel in my bones that I was right. "Olivia keeps dancing around the question each time I ask about the money. She's the queen of deflection. I can't get a straight answer out of her lying mouth. Experience tells me when people can't be straight with you, it's because they're fucking trying to hide something."

I felt Jilly's despair as if it were my own as she nodded in agreement, bemoaning, "That fucking bastard...the things he did to me...were *inhuman*! How could they do this to us? We're fucking people for God's sakes!"

I soothed her with understanding murmurs but I didn't have an answer that would satisfy because I was just as bewildered as Jilly. "I wish I knew. All I can figure is that they're soulless. How else can someone do such awful things to another human being?"

Jilly nodded but I knew it wasn't enough. We were all confused by how this happened.

"I can't believe I was stupid as to believe that any of this was real. They used us for the one thing they wanted and now they're just going to throw us away?"

"No," I returned with savage conviction "they are not going to throw us away because we aren't going to let them."

Jilly's frantic confusion colored her voice. "What

do you mean? We're stuck here. They're guarding us with men packing guns. How the hell are we supposed to get out? It's not like they're going to let us walk out the front door."

"Yeah, but they don't know that I can get out. And that's exactly what we're going to do as soon as I find Tana. Dylan is a few doors down. I think they keep all the girls on this floor because it makes sense. Organized, even."

Jilly sniffed and wiped her nose with the back of her hand. "Yeah? I guess so. But how are we going to escape? I'm sure the grounds are guarded by dogs with big teeth and men with really big guns."

"I thought that too but I've been listening to every sound this house makes and I've never heard any dogs. I think they've just got the guards we've seen. They don't think we're capable of pushing against a locked door. Their biggest mistake is under-estimating us."

"I don't want to die," Jilly whispered, her big eyes fearful. "Please don't let me die, Nicole."

I wasn't a fucking hero by any stretch of the imagination but I couldn't let their story end here "I won't," I promised. "As soon as I find Tana, we're getting the fuck out of here. All of us."

Jilly nodded, taking my promise to heart. She

sniffed again, drawing her knees up to her chest. "Did your buyer...did he hurt you?"

I swallowed as I nodded. "Did yours?"

She answered with an ashamed nod. I held her tightly as she cried silent tears on my shoulder. I hated these people more than I ever hated Carla, which was a pretty significant benchmark. I hungered for vengeance but I wasn't stupid.

We were a bunch of kids no one cared about. How could we do anything to affect Madame Moirai's operation? We were gnats buzzing around a giant. As much as I wanted to smash this network into the ground, getting out alive was more important.

I pulled away, wiping at Jilly's tears, feeling so much older when we were the same age. "Listen, I need you to pretend that nothing has changed. I don't want them to get suspicious and increase security, okay?" She nodded and I continued with my instructions. "I'm going to leave you now so I can find Tana. If I find Tana, we're busting out tonight. If I can't find Tana, we have one more night before our five days is officially up. I have a feeling that's when all hell's going to break loose. Right now, Olivia is trying to force me to accept my elevation but that's never going to happen. Once she realizes I'm not going to budge, my fate will be the same as everyone else's and I'll give you one guess as to what they might be."

Jilly swallowed. "They're going to kill us?"

"Or sell us to a brothel out of the country."

"Jesus," she breathed in fear. "Please no."

"It's not going to happen," I told her. "We're getting out."

Jilly nodded, bolstered by my fierce determination. "Okay, I trust you."

I felt the weight of those words settle on my shoulders. Fuck, when did I become a savior? I was just a kid with a bad attitude. I never thought I'd become the kind of person who others looked to as a champion.

Fate was a cruel bitch.

I couldn't walk away with Dylan, Jilly and Tana lost to this place. Of all the things I'd have to live through, the shame of abandoning them wasn't something I'd ever survive and I knew it.

With a few final words of encouragement, I left Jilly and slipped back into the hall, creeping through the shadows, mindful of every step, every sound. I hoped and prayed I found Tana's room so we could ditch this nightmare tonight but I ran out of locked doors. Worry seized me as I realized Tana was not on the same floor as we were.

Where was she?

I made my way to Dylan's room and let myself in. I wasn't surprised to see her awake and waiting for me.

"Did you find Jilly," she asked in a hushed tone. At my nod, she followed with, "What about Tana? Or anyone else?"

"I only found Jilly," I answered, worried. "I have a bad feeling about this. Why wouldn't they put her on the same floor as us? There are plenty of other rooms just like ours. Something must've went wrong? Or bad? Or...I don't know."

Dylan worried her bottom lip with her teeth, admitting she shared the same concerns. "It doesn't make sense to keep her someplace else unless..."

"Don't say it," I said, not wanting to go there but it was in the back of my mind. Tana had been so scared that not even the Xanax had managed to completely calm her down. What if she'd freaked out with her buyer and he threw her back to Madame Moirai with the demand for a refund? How would Tana be punished for something like that? "Maybe she's downstairs somewhere. We don't need to jump to conclusions."

"C'mon, you're thinking exactly what I'm thinking," Dylan persisted. "If anyone could've pushed someone's buttons it would've been that girl. She never should've signed the deal."

"None of us should've signed that contract," I corrected with a short hiss. My fear for Tana made me prickly. Or maybe it was just Dylan. "We all made a shitty choice. Try to remember that."

"Yeah, of course, I'm just saying, out of all of us... she wasn't mentally ready for whatever was going to happen. All I can say is that if her buyer did to her what mine did to me...that girl would've killed herself."

I wanted to cry for all of us. For being stupid, naive girls who thought they were more badass than they actually were. Fuck, Madame Moirai had picked her marks well and that made me hate the shadowy woman all the more.

"Is Jilly okay?" Dylan asked.

"As much as can be expected," I answered. "She's pretty traumatized. Like we all are to some degree."

"If I ever see my buyer again, I'll fucking kill him," Dylan promised. I believed her. If we had more time and the resources, I'd gladly help her but we didn't have that option.

However, rage was good. It kept the shame and anguish away, at least for the time being. I needed Dylan focused. "We need to get out of here first. Then, we can talk about revenge."

I wanted to get as far away from this place as possible. I didn't know how to put my life back together but I'd focus on that problem after I was safe.

I needed to get back to my room. I turned to Dylan. "I'm going back to my room. We have one more night before our five days is up. I need to try and find Tana. Tomorrow night, be ready. One way or another, we're leaving this fucked up place."

Dylan nodded. "I'll be ready."

I knew she would be. I quietly let myself out, relocked Dylan's door and found my own. I let myself in and locked the door. I hid my bobby pins and climbed back in bed but sleep didn't find me right away. I was too bound up with worry for Tana. My gut told me something bad had happened but I didn't want to believe it. I wanted to cling to the hope that Tana was just on a different level of the house, even though common sense told me that was inefficient.

We were nothing but rats in a cage to them.

Like Dylan, I thirsted for someone's head on a

plate but realistically, how could I pull that off? I would have to settle for simply getting out.

It didn't feel as satisfying but hell, at least I'd be alive to bitch about it.

Tana...please be all right.

17

Olivia didn't show up until lunch but when she did, she came with a tray loaded with entrees that made my mouth water after the disgusting oatmeal punishment. I tried to hide my reaction but my gaze kept straying to the platter, the smell of a perfectly grilled hamburger with fries teasing my nose and causing my stomach to yowl like a cat in heat.

"You must be very hungry," Olivia said, placing the tray near me with a welcoming gesture and a sickly sweet smile that reminded me of a wolf eyeing the rabbit. "I can only imagine. I hate oatmeal. How about you?"

So, we were completely ignoring the fact that she'd served up that gross shit as a punishment? *Okay, fine. Whatever.*

I ignored her question and took a savage bite from the thick hamburger, adding a few fries into my gob as well. My rage percolated beneath the surface but if I was telling Dylan to control herself, I had to as well. But fuck, it was hard. Each time I looked at her face, I wanted to put my fist into it.

"Have you given any more thought to Madame Moirai's generous offer?"

It was a good thing thought bubbles didn't erupt over my head. Madame Moirai could shove her offer up her pie-hole but I kept my hot words tempered. I shrugged, as if I were contemplating the idea. "I have questions," I admitted, scooping a spoonful of macaroni salad into my mouth, taking a moment to spit out the sweet pickles. Further proof that these people were monsters — dill pickles were the only acceptable choices for a macaroni salad.

"Excellent, that's what I'm here for — to answer any questions you may have," Olivia said, folding her hands neatly in her lap with an expectant expression. "Please, whenever you're ready."

"Well, I'm kinda starved, so sorry if I talk with my mouth full," I said with a tiny slip of acid in my tone. Olivia smiled in understanding. Of course, she was, oh so patient when I was being cooperative. Did she get an extra cut for the girls who agreed to accept their elevation offer? This machine was greased by money and everyone involved was guilty as fuck. I wiped my mouth with the linen napkin and tried to ignore the wave of guilt knowing that Dylan and Jilly were choking down slops while I was being treated like a captive queen. "Look, I've had a little time to think about the offer and maybe I was careless in saying that Henri...well, you know, but it's all been really jarring. It's not like this was a trip to the mall. Sometimes it's hard to wrap your brain around it all."

Olivia bent her head in understanding. "It's a lot to absorb."

That's an understatement. "Yeah, exactly. So, let's just say that I was interested in taking the deal. What's my cut?"

Oliva chuckled as if impressed. "Look at you, straight to business," she said, flattering me. "You constantly surprise us. I'm sure that's why Mr. Benoit is taken with you. Your personality is so unique."

I forced down the bile rising in my throat, pushing my food up my trachea. I took a moment to slug down some water before saying, "Well, that's me, unique to a T. But back to the money — by my calculations, I'm due sixty grand but I haven't actually *seen* the money yet. You gotta understand why I'm a little apprehensive to take a new deal from Madame Moirai when she hasn't paid up on the first. That just seems like bad business, you know?"

Olivia's smile chilled as she said, "Of course, perfectly normal to have concerns. However, if you recall, your contract states that the money is deposited one week *after* you've left Madame Moirai's employ. It takes time to process the paperwork."

"Right, clandestine sex work must be murder on the accountants," I murmured with fake commiseration. "I can only imagine."

"Yes, well, strict protocols keep everyone moving in the same direction," she said, pressing on. "As to your compensation, the same deal applies. Whatever the buyer offers, Madame Moirai takes her forty percent and you collect the rest. It's all very similar to what you signed before. Very straight-forward."

Not even. "I hate to be a stickler for details but nowhere in the contract that I signed did it say anything about being locked up. I feel like I'm in a prison," I said.

"I'm sorry for the seemingly overly-cautious protocols," Olivia said, affecting an apologetic expression, adding, "but it's all coming to an end soon."

"Yes, today is the fifth day."

"Indeed it is."

"So, if I don't take the deal — as generous it is — my assumption is that you'll return my original clothes and all my belongings and I can go home?"

"Of course," Oliva answered but her tone had flattened, which told me she was lying through her goddamn perfect teeth. "But I urge you to consider Madame Moirai's offer. I can tell you with complete honesty, that it's not often auction girls such as yourself get elevated."

"Yeah but I really don't have many details and it's hard to make a decision with such murky information."

"What else is there to know?" Olivia asked, mildly perturbed.

"Oh, well, lots. For example, in the original contract, there was a specific time frame. How long does Mr. Benoit think he will want my company? A week, a month? I mean, let's get real, I haven't even graduated high school yet. My mom might not notice if I don't come back but the school certainly will. Kids can't just stop going to school. It's the law."

"You'd be surprised."

Well, that was scary as fuck. "What do you mean?"

She waved away my question as if I shouldn't worry about those types of details. "Arrangements can be made to take care of any questions that may arise from your absence."

"Like home-schooling or something?"

Olivia's irritation returned. "Yes, something like that."

She was a terrible liar. They didn't fucking care if I never went back to school. I was just a vagina with legs. They made me want to vomit. How did someone get to the point where they no longer felt anything for another human being?

Somewhere along the way, someone had scooped Olivia's soul out, leaving her a hollowed-out shell, which was probably exactly as Madame Moirai preferred.

There seemed only one answer for that kind of programming.

"You were elevated, weren't you?" I asked, circling back around to the question I asked the other day that she sidestepped. I didn't wait for her answer. "Was your buyer kind? Was he a gentle lover? Someone you didn't mind whoring for? My guess is that he didn't assault or beat you. Otherwise, why would you agree to elevate when you could've walked away with a fat check and free of this nightmare?" I paused a minute before asking, "Do you ever think of the life you were forced to leave behind? Did you ever actually get paid?"

"We aren't talking about me," Olivia snapped, showing real emotion for the first time. She curled her palms into fists as she took a minute to compose herself. After a heartbeat, she met my gaze with her narrowed one. "It would seem that you haven't had enough time to consider what an honor Mr. Benoit is offering you. I was premature in rewarding you. That won't happen again."

"Well, actually, according to my contract, I get to go home today so no more oatmeal for me," I reminded Olivia. "Or has that changed, too?"

Olivia rose and took my platter from me. I wasn't finished but that was all I was going to get. "I'll return when you're ready to talk sensibly."

She left my room and it locked behind her, presumably by a guard.

"Psycho bitch," I muttered. Who had Olivia been before Madame Moirai turned her into this sex trafficking auto-bot? It was pretty obvious by Olivia's reaction, she'd been an auction girl at some point, too. *Boo-hoo*. I couldn't whip up enough empathy for the victim Olivia had been once because she was now working side by side with the devil and that made her just as evil.

No matter my stubborn defiance, they had the upper hand.

I went to the small window and peered outside. The gray skies mirrored the fear threatening to sour my resolve. It was a long drop from the window to the ground. There was nothing but trees for miles. We were somewhere in the middle of fucking nowhere.

No one to hear kidnapped girls scream for help.

I pressed against the cold glass, closing my eyes, seeking some kind of reserve strength. Panic and despair were the enemy. I couldn't give in to either. The girls were relying on me to get them out. I opened my eyes, trying to memorize every small detail I could see from my limited view. A subtle break in the tree line caught my eye. That must be the road, I realized. It wasn't exactly close but if there was a road, there was a chance out of here. I craned against the glass, trying to see more but I couldn't.

It's okay, I told myself. The road gave me hope. I

knew the direction we would run when we busted out of this place tonight. Having a plan, even a vague one, was enough to calm my racing heart and quiet the fearful whimpering in the back of my head.

I wasn't going to die here and I wasn't going back to Henri.

That monster could choke on a dick for all I cared. He deserved far worse but I'd settle for something embarrassing that still got the job done. The reality was that I'd probably never get the justice I craved but there was some comfort in imagining it happening.

Just thinking of Henri made my skin crawl. I pushed away from the window and went to the shower, turning it on full blast and hot enough to burn.

I welcomed the needle-like pain of the spray as it pelted my body. I braced myself against the wall, letting the water wash over me. There wasn't enough water in the world to wash away the horror of what he'd done to me but when I thought of Dylan and the horrific bruises all over her body or the haunted look in Jilly's eyes, I knew somehow — as shocking as it was — I'd gotten off light.

Henri could've done so much more to me. That

closet of horrors came back to jeer at me and I knew without a doubt that Henri had probably killed someone for fun at some point. Somewhere there's an auction girl who hadn't gotten the version of Henri that he played with me and had died at his hands.

Henri had paid the fine and then, signed up for a new auction.

Girls like me meant nothing to people like Henri — we were throwaways.

Tears pricked my eyes. *Someone would miss me if I never came home,* I told myself. Lora would cry for me.

But even as I desperately clung to the hope that Lora would press for answers, I knew she'd never ask the *right* questions because she had no idea what I'd done to put myself in this situation. Fuck, I should've told her. I should've swallowed my pride and told Lora, even as a fail-safe but I didn't.

If I didn't come home, eventually, she'd assume I ran away and she'd let anger override her grief. Then, I'd become just a footnote in her life, a troubling but distant question that was never answered.

I let the tears fall down my cheeks. I sobbed quietly beneath the spray, needing to purge some of this rage and fear if I were going to have the strength to do what needed to be done tonight.

Tonight, we would either get out or die trying.

At this point, I wouldn't accept anything less.

Henri — or anyone like him — was never touching me again.

18

Just as I expected, Olivia didn't return with my belongings and a stiff goodbye because the fifth day came and went with no change in my circumstances. Also, I didn't even get oatmeal for dinner.

Olivia through she could starve me into compliance. *Good luck with that, bitch.* I pulled my bobby pins free from their hiding spot and quickly and quietly picked the lock. I was getting pretty damn good at it by this point. The house was still, which made me wonder if Olivia even stayed here with the chattel. This house wasn't a residence, it was a holding arena.

I popped into Dylan's room. She was awake and ready. "You think it's no accident that they don't give us anything but soft booties for our feet?" she said. "Joke's on them, I'll walk on glass to get out of here."

I nodded, agreeing. "I'm going to check on Jilly, then make another sweep for Tana. If I can't find Tana..." I gulped at the implication "We'll leave without her."

Dylan understood. "Be careful," she warned, not because she was overcome with emotion for me but because she knew I was her only way out. I accepted her advice and slipped from the room.

I did the same for Jilly. Like Dylan, she was wide awake and ready to run. She practically vibrated with nervous energy. "What if you can't find Tana?" she asked, the fear in her eyes reflecting my own. "What are you going to do?"

"We'll have to leave without her," I answered. "But I'm going to do my damndest to find her. I'm going to check the other levels."

"Oh my God, that's so dangerous! You might get caught! Please don't. If she's not on this floor, she's probably not even here," Jilly said, chewing her fingernail. "If you get caught, we're all screwed."

"I won't get caught," I assured her. "I'm pretty good at getting around without being seen. Trust me, okay? Just be ready to run when I come from you and don't make a fucking sound."

Jilly nodded and I left her room. Even though I knew Tana wasn't in an unlocked room, I checked them anyway. The rooms were exactly like the rest, a bare-bones room, devoid of luxury but serviceable. They were also empty. However, given that there were six rooms on this floor, I was shaken by the realization that at some point, all the rooms might've been filled with desperate girls.

If these walls could talk, what atrocities would they reveal in hushed whispers?

I paused in the shadows, listening for footsteps. My ears pricked at a distant sound and I realized a guard was on patrol. I slipped into one of the empty unlocked rooms and waited for the sound of his footsteps to pass me by.

My heart hammered in my chest at the threat of being discovered. Everything rode on me to get us out. I couldn't get caught now. With my luck it would be that asshole who wanted to murder me for funsies. No doubt he'd delight in sticking a nightstick up my ass for my smart mouth.

I waited a good five minutes to ensure that the guard was gone from the floor, then exited the room. I peered into the darkness and saw the guard already downstairs, disappearing into another area. I needed to get past him and search the rest of the house. My ears strained for the slightest noise that gave away a guard on patrol. Thankfully, they had no reason to disguise their presence and they weren't concerned with being silent like I was.

By my count, it seemed there were three guards on patrol and they were pooling in another room, after their required patrol.

Thankfully, Madame Moirai's guard staff were stupid, lazy fucks because they didn't seem to think we were capable of trying to escape.

I made it downstairs and followed the sound of their voices until I was pressed against the opposite wall and able to hear their every word.

I recognized the voice of the asshole and suppressed a shudder.

"I don't know what's so special about that little bitch in room five. If it were up to me, I'd put her in the ground."

"Well, it's not up to you," another voice growled a reminder. "Keep your hands to yourself. She's going to elevate. If Madame Moirai discovers you've done anything to fuck up her plans, you'll be the one in the ground."

"Fuck, I know that," grumbled Asshole. "I'm just saying, I don't get why she's so special. She ain't got that great of tits and her face is just meh. Hell, I think that little bitch in room three is a sweeter piece of ass and she's less trouble."

Asshole was talking about Jilly. *Fucker*.

"Well, we don't get paid to make those decisions," the other said. "Did you check the locks?"

"Tight as a drum, as always," asshole sighed with annoyance that he was even asked. "Are you kidding me, those scared little bitches are afraid of their own shadows at this point."

The fuck we are.

Light laughter followed. "Yeah, that one in Room Two really got it good. Surprised she even came back in one piece at all," a new voice chimed in. "Hell, the last time a girl came in like that, she bled out by morning. Gotta hand it to her, she's a scraper."

"She's proven she can take a hit," Asshole agreed, adding, "it's a shame, though. That one had great tits. I wouldn't mind going a few rounds with her. I don't get why these rich pricks gotta tear up good merch. It's like pissing in a goddamn Ferrari, you know?"

I wanted to throw up. They were talking about us like we were nothing. I balled my fists to keep from running in there and attacking the first one I could reach.

"It's their merch. They can do what they want

with it. Even if it means pissing on a fine piece of ass."

Asshole asked, "Hey, what do you think about paying Room Two a visit tonight? Sleeping beauty might like a little action before lights out, you know?"

"Keep your dick in your pants, Darryl," the voice ground out in annoyance, as if this was something Asshole suggested often. "The last thing we need is your fucking DNA everywhere. Stop thinking with your fucking cock or else you're going to find yourself in a world of hurt."

"All right, all right," Darryl grumbled, backing down. "I was just saying...could be fun."

So Asshole's name was Darryl. I filed away that information. Not sure for what, but I was collecting anything and everything that might prove useful later.

"It's your turn to deal."

They were playing cards to pass the time. That worked in my favor. I'd heard enough. I carefully backed away, and crept down the opposite hall, my eyes wide and wary. I was pretty sure it was only those three guards but I wasn't willing to stake my life on it.

The house was massive. I felt the ticking of the clock pressing against me. I searched room upon room, finding most empty, as if they were never used but others I found dressed with fine furnishings like a showroom. I was starting to piece together how the house was used. The furnished rooms were likely where the potential clients were given the sales pitch. The rest of the rooms were for storage or left empty.

I bypassed the elevator and found the staircase leading to the subfloor. I recognized the difference in the smell. Even as finely as this house was made, the subfloor had a subtle dank smell that reminded me of mildew hiding in the walls. I started to shake, remembering the auction.

I hadn't taken the Xanax. My memory was crystal-clear and agonizingly vivid but I was grateful I hadn't let Olivia talk me into it swallowing that pill.

I found the room where the auction was held.

The center stage was empty, the lights off. Smoked glass panes of glass surrounded the center. Chains with manacles hung silent from the ceiling. We four had been hung like sides of beef in this place, twisting and turning helplessly as men hid behind privacy glass to bid in complete anonymity.

Tears pricked my eyes but I held them back. Now wasn't the time. Tana wasn't in here. I backed out of the hateful room and continued my search.

The subfloor was a maze of rooms, some functional and some empty, similar to upstairs.

This entire house was a machine with one purpose — the sale of young girls and maybe boys. Hell, I didn't know if Madame Moirai specialized in one gender or was an equal opportunity predator. I didn't want to know.

The smell of humiliation and despair clung to my nostrils even though the floors looked immaculate. Once, in my mom's brief hippy phase, she'd hooked up with this supposed guru who could see energy and read people's auras. Of the long line of my mother's boyfriends, Byron had been the least offensive, but he'd been weird as fuck.

He told me — while high as a kite on Ayahuasca — that everything retained residual energy, which was why people thought houses were haunted.

"It's just energy, man," he'd said, gazing up at the cracked and water damaged ceiling of our shit-hole apartment as if he were counting stars. "Energy is everything."

I'd thought he was full of shit and his brains had been eaten out by all the drugs he did but maybe he'd been right. I could feel a darkness clinging to the walls, seeping into the house's pores, oozing from each crack and crevice. As if I could hear the screams of girls' long gone echoing in this basement, crying out in terror.

Fear was a powerful energy. It definitely left its mark.

I ground out the tears in my eyes and kept going, determined to make it out of this place alive. I wouldn't be like those other girls. I wouldn't end up in the ground or at the mercy of Darryl the Sociopathic Guard.

One last door to check and then I had to admit that Tana wasn't here. I tried the door. It was locked. Wild hope flickered in my heart. They only kept the girls in locked rooms. I pulled out my bobby pins and impatiently worked the lock. My fingers were clumsy with my frantic need to open that door.

Finally, the lock clicked and the door opened. Darkness blanketed the room but I could tell right away there was something distinctly different about this room. The chill in the air was unlike any of the others. It was downright frosty in this room. "Tana?" I whispered into the darkness, hoping against hope she was not in this room. An odd smell tickled my nostrils.

My fingers searched along the wall for a light switch. There weren't any windows in this room because not a shred of light pierced the suffocating pitch black. I found the switch and flooded the room with blazing, bright light.

I gasped in shock, shrinking against the wall when I realized what this room was — a fucking morgue.

Stainless steel cabinets lined the wall and three metal autopsy tables gleamed in the harsh light, one of which had a covered figure, a white sheet blanketing the form.

I didn't want to look.

Please, don't be under that fucking sheet.

But I had to know.

I approached the shrouded figure, dragging my feet, my mind shrieking that I was alone with a corpse.

I reached for the sheet with shaking fingers. The sturdy linen slipped from my numb hands and I had to reach again. This time I managed to slowly pull back the sheet to see who was beneath that sea of white linen.

Time stopped along with my breath.

Nooooooooo!

No! No! No!

Tana, with her bright ruby curls and pale as milk skin, eyes closed, lay on that gurney, silenced forever.

I bit my lip to stop from screaming. Mottled

bruises marred most of her skin, telling a story of a brutal and painful death. Even her private parts were abused. I glanced away, nearly crumpling in on myself at the knowledge that this sweet girl had been tortured before her end.

What penalty or fine had her buyer given to Madame Moirai for this crime? No amount of money would forgive what'd been done to Tana.

I'd hardly known her but seeing her on that slab, knowing how she'd suffered, knowing how we'd all been duped, made me see red. I wanted blood. I wanted justice. I wanted...fuck, I wanted to grab Tana and drag her lifeless body out of this hell-hole and make sure she was given a proper burial so that she could be mourned like she deserved.

She'd been a good kid — not like the rest of us.

She hadn't been a throwaway. Somewhere she had a grandmother who would never understand why her beloved Tana would never come home.

Even if that poor woman's brain was being destroyed by a horrible disease, she'd sense that something wasn't right.

And it wasn't.

Holy fuck, nothing would ever be right again.

Goddamn it! Everything was wrong with the world when people like Madame Moirai could callously collect broken kids and sell them like they were less than nothing.

I smoothed Tana's curls, tears streaming down my face. "I'm so sorry," I whispered. "I'm so, so sorry."

There was nothing more I could say. I gently replaced the sheet over her face, wiping at my nose and willing the tears to stop.

I'd found Tana and she was never leaving this place.

But we would have to if we didn't want to end up on the slabs next to Tana.

However, as I took one final look at Tana's shrouded body, I made a vow:

I was going to destroy everyone associated with the auction.

I didn't know how...but I knew I wouldn't rest until someone paid with blood for Tana — and every other girl who'd landed on this slab for the crime of hoping for a better life.

Fuck you, Madame Moirai. I'm coming for you.

19

As I left the makeshift morgue, I went back into the rooms to find anything I could use as a weapon but as I was searching, I realized I had exactly what I needed to create the kind of distraction that would enable us to get out.

I returned to the morgue, my gaze avoiding Tana's body, and found more sheets in the steel cabinet. Balling them up, I stuffed them into corners of the room and saturated them with embalming fluid.

Thank you, Freshman Chemistry 101.

Then, I did the same thing to the auction room until each corner had a potential fire hazard just waiting for a match to go crazy.

When I found a lighter tucked away in a desk drawer — God bless fucking smokers — I took one final look around, mouthed a silent goodbye to Tana, and then covering my mouth and nose went about lighting each and every one of those balls of retribution with grim satisfaction as they immediately went up in flames.

I hustled out of the subfloor, pausing only long enough to make sure that the guards were still playing cards, then bounded up the stairs to slip into Dylan's room.

This place was probably equipped with a fire alarm, which I was counting on, but even if it didn't, the fire downstairs would soon enough make itself known with billowing smoke.

Dylan looked to me, ready to run, just as I told her to be.

I held my fingers up to my lips as I listened.

Suddenly, a loud alarm pealed through the house, seconds before a loud explosion jarred the floor beneath our feet. We steadied ourselves as the house rattled. Holy shit, I might've used too much embalming fluid because the mini-explosions popping off downstairs were growing in intensity as the heat climbed.

"Was that you?" She pointed at me and I nodded.

"Fucking savage," Dylan said with blood-thirsty

approval. "Let's get the hell out of here before the whole house goes up in a ball of fire."

"You took the words right out of my mouth," I quipped, waiting to hear the guards rushing from their card game to run downstairs. The thunder of feet and panicked shouting signaled it was time to make our move. I motioned for Dylan to follow as I opened the door.

I heard fire extinguishers going off as they tried to battle the blaze before it overtook the house. They were too busy to worry about us. The last thing Madame Moirai wanted was the cops and fire department to show up so they had to handle things on their own. *Good luck with that.* I hoped they burned.

I opened Jilly's door and she quickly joined us.

"Where's Tana?" Jilly asked but I couldn't tell her right now. If I tried, I would break down and I couldn't afford to do that. Not yet. I shook my head and gestured for them to follow.

Jilly and Dylan fell in behind me and we made our way down the stairs, staying to the shadows, listening for footsteps coming our way. We burst from the back door and hit the ground running. My frantic heartbeat was deafening as our feet ate up the dirt, mindless of the rocks and sticks grinding into our skin. Nothing mattered but getting free. We'd all gladly suffer torn up feet if it meant escaping Madame Moirai.

We didn't look back. We didn't stop. My lungs were ready to explode but I kept pushing. There wasn't nearly enough distance between us and them to stop yet.

I ran with single-minded focus. I couldn't worry if the girls fell behind. I envisioned the road and kept running in the direction that I saw from my window. Bracken brambles tore at my skin and darkened trees pressed against the starry sky as hidden roots caught my toe and ripped my toenail free.

I didn't have time to scream. I barely felt the pain.

Finally, what seemed like forever, we crashed out of the woods to land on a desolate highway. I stumbled to my knees, ripping the flimsy pajama bottoms and skinning the flesh raw and bloody but I didn't care.

Dylan and Jilly were seconds behind me. The sound of our harsh breathing as we gasped for air filled the night. It was then, I realized Jilly was sobbing.

"Where's Tana?" she cried. "Where is she?"

I couldn't form words yet. My tongue was furred

and my throat aching. I just shook my head, tears welling in my eyes.

"She wasn't downstairs either?" Dylan asked, bracketing her hands on her hips as she tried to breathe.

"Tana..." I gulped, shaking my head, knowing I had to tell them. "She's dead."

"What?" Jilly breathed in horror. "How do you know?"

"I saw her," I answered, letting my gaze roll to the skies as I tried to keep the tears at bay. The image of Tana on that slab would haunt me forever. "They have a makeshift morgue downstairs and I saw her. She was," I gulped, hating the image seared into my brain "she was beaten to death. I don't know when she died but she's gone."

Dylan swore under her breath, looking away but not before I caught the sheen in her eyes. "Goddamn motherfuckers," she spat "they all ought to rot in hell for what they've done."

"She was so scared," Jilly recalled, her eyes spilling with tears "she pleaded with them to take her back, that she'd changed her mind. I was the last to see her before they dragged her out of the room. She was crying when they took her away. Not even the Xanax could help her calm down."

I remembered.

"What did they do to her?" Jilly cried, the question rhetorical.

But I didn't have time to answer. A car was coming our way. Hope leaped into my throat until I realized the car was driving too fast to be good. "Hide!" I said in a harsh voice as we melted back into the forest, dropping to our bellies to avoid being seen from the road.

Jilly was confused, tears still glistening on her cheek. "Why are we hiding?" she asked, looking to both Dylan and me. "We need a ride out of here."

Dylan was grim as she answered, "It was them. They're looking for us."

I nodded. "They must've put the fire out and realized we weren't in our rooms or they realized there was no way they were going to be able to put out that fire and ran to save their own asses. Either way, they've figured out that we're loose and we can't afford to be seen."

"What are we going to do?" Jilly asked, fearful.

"We're going to walk, stick to the forest line. Eventually, we'll reach a spot where we can safely find a ride," I said.

"Do you know where we are?" Jilly asked.

"No," I admitted, plus it was dark. Nothing

looked the same under cover of night. "But all roads lead somewhere, right? Do you remember how long the car ride took when Mr. Personality picked you up?"

"About an hour?" Dylan estimated.

"Same for me."

Jilly nodded, agreeing.

"Okay, so we know we can't be too far from the city. There's gotta be a town close enough to walk to. We'll try to get a ride back to the city from there." I spoke with more confidence than I felt. Dylan was still pretty banged up and Jilly looked like she was about to have a nervous break down any minute but we had to keep moving. I didn't need to tell them that either we kept moving or we got swept up in Madame Moirai's net again.

"I can hot-wire a car if we find one," Dylan piped in, agreeing to my plan. She squared her shoulders as she said, "Let's do it. I'm no stranger to walking."

I wasn't either but I was very glad that at least one of us could boost a car. I could pick a lock but I'd never messed around with grand theft auto.

We set out with a brisk pace, ignoring the pain in our feet and the bruises on our bodies. Silence wound itself around us, our own thoughts holding us captive as walked. None of us wanted to talk. There was too much in our heads, too much to process. We were numb to it. Maybe in shock. I felt miles away from the girl who'd signed away her life for the false promise of a better one. I didn't really know how to return to my old life.

I didn't know if it was safe to ever return.

All Tana had wanted was a secure future for her grandmother. She hadn't even thought of using the money for herself.

I'd wanted to get away from my mother.

I had no idea what hopes and plans Jilly or Dylan had prompted them to take the deal.

Fear gripped me as I faced a terrifying unknown with even less than I had started with. Taking a big risk had seemed worth it for an even bigger payout but now we had less than nothing and we couldn't go home.

We would end up putting everyone who cared about us into harm's way if we tried. For me, that was Lora. I couldn't handle the thought of Lora getting swept up in this ugly mess. It wasn't her fault and I wouldn't subject her to any of this.

What have I done?

How was it possible that less than a week ago, I'd been sitting in my room, studying for an English exam and now I was running for my life?

"She's never going to let us go," Jilly said, echoing my own thoughts. "We're loose ends. If we talked Madame Moirai could go to jail."

"Do you know who Madame Moirai is?" Dylan returned with too much sarcasm for what we'd all been through. "'Cause I sure as hell don't. Who are we going to tell? Who would believe us?"

"Shouldn't we go to the cops?" Jilly asked.

"And say what? 'Hi Officer, we signed a contract with a stranger to sell our virginity for a shit-ton of money but then that stranger turned on us and tried to have us killed after we'd served our purpose?' Yeah, it doesn't really have a catchy ring to it. No cop is going to touch that with a ten-foot pole," Dylan said. "We're on our own."

"You don't know that the cops can't help us. We're kids for godsakes" Jilly said, panic returning to her voice. "Holy fuck, doesn't anyone care about us at all?"

"No," I answered quietly, meeting her gaze. "No one cares about people like us. That's how Madame Moirai gets away with this shit. You think she's going to go after the prom queen or the captain of the debate club? No, she goes after kids who are desperate because the world turned its back on them a long time ago. It's kinda brilliant, actually."

"It's not fair," Jilly cried. "And she's not fucking brilliant, she's an opportunistic sadist."

"With a head for business," Dylan added with a dark expression.

I cast a look to Dylan that said, *shut the fuck up*, but only muttered to Jilly, "Tell that to Tana. Fair is a word that never applied to us."

I didn't want to talk anymore. My heart hurt. My soul felt broken. I just wanted to find someplace safe to hole up and sleep for a few days. I had no idea where that might be but I knew I couldn't go back so I had to keep moving forward. "Just keep walking. We need to find a place to hide out for a while until we figure out what to do next."

"I know a place we can go, back in the city," Dylan volunteered gruffly. At my surprise, she scowled. "Look, I'm not interested in holding hands and becoming besties are anything but we're fucking stuck together for the time being so we might as well pool our resources, right?"

"All cops aren't bad," Jilly persisted. "We should go straight to the first police station and tell them what's happened to us."

Jilly desperately wanted someone to save us. Someone bigger, stronger and with more resources but I agreed with Dylan, no one was going to help us. They'd take one look at us and make a quick judgment, assuming we were lying or trying to pull off a con. Or worse, they'd arrest us for being whores because prostitution was still illegal.

"We need to lay low for a few days," I told Jilly, being gentle because Dylan was not. "After we make sure that we're not being followed, maybe we can approach a cop but not until we know that we can trust them."

It was a compromise that worked for Jilly. She nodded, conceding, "I guess that makes sense. But you promise we'll go to the cops in a few days?"

"As soon as we're able," I answered, dancing around the promise.

"Fine," Jilly reluctantly agreed. To Dylan, she asked, "Where's this place?"

"It's an underground for runaways. You have to know someone to get in. Lucky for us, I know the right people but let me do the talking."

We accepted the plan, loose as it was because we didn't have a choice.

We were an unlikely trio, bound by trauma and grief, none of us too happy about it. We knew the rules of the street — there was safety in numbers — and we needed all the protection we could gather if we were going to dodge Madame Moirai's grasping fingers.

The shadowy woman had a long fucking reach.

For all we knew she had cops on the payroll, too.

I agreed with Dylan...we couldn't really trust cops.

We could only trust each other.

And even that was sketchy.

Fuck, we were probably screwed.

20

"I have to stop," Jilly declared with a pained expression. "I just need a minute, please. I have to sit down for a second or I'm going to collapse."

Both Dylan and I stopped, neither of us wanting to slow down but we could see that Jilly was at her breaking point and we didn't want to end up carrying her. "Fine, we can take a short break," I said, gesturing for everyone to hide in the tree line, away from the road. I wasn't taking any chances even though we hadn't seen another car pass by in almost two hours.

Dylan eased herself to the ground, grimacing as she settled. Of all of us, Dylan was the most visibly hurt. The bruising stood out in garish, mottled patches across her body, up her arms and her face.

Yet, she trudged on like a soldier, as single-mindedly focused as me and I had to respect her strength.

I mean, the girl had an iron will that rivaled my own and that was saying something. It's probably why we butted heads so much, too.

Jilly shivered and we crowded around her for warmth. Hugging her knees to her chest, she sat shaking between us for a good two minutes before the quivering in her body slowly stopped.

An owl hooted in the distance, echoing into the stillness. "The forest is creepy at night," Dylan said, glancing around, peering into the darkness. "The quiet gives me the heebie-jeebies."

"I don't mind it," Jilly said. "Reminds me a foster home when I was younger. They were the nicest couple I'd ever met. Different from the rest. They lived out in the country. The crickets helped me sleep at night."

"What happened to them?" I asked.

"They died in a car accident," Jilly answered dully. "Just when I thought I'd maybe found a place to call home with nice people, they went and died. All of their fosters were thrown back into the system and that was the last nice place I ever had."

Dylan nodded, Jilly's story seeming to resonate but she didn't share.

"Sometimes I used to wish child services would show up and remove me from my mother's custody but it never happened. We moved around too much for them to catch us," I said. "Carla had a knack for knowing when they were starting to close in, asking questions. Then, suddenly, we were moving again."

"I don't know what's worse, a shitty foster parent or a shitty parent. They both suck," Dylan said. "My dad was a mean drunk but he wasn't much better sober. I didn't wait for child services to rescue me. I bailed on my own. Been on my own since I was fifteen."

We fell silent, digesting each other's stories. My eyes burned. The adrenaline rush that'd fueled our mad dash to the road had long since evaporated, leaving me drained. I winced at the crusted blood on my big toe where the toenail was ripped off and knew I needed to clean it or it was going to get infected. *Tough titty, I guess.* Nowhere to clean up around here. I struggled to my feet, stiff from the cold ground. "We should get moving," I said.

Jilly didn't look happy but climbed to her feet. She cast a concerned look toward Dylan. "Are you okay to keep going?"

"Don't worry about me, worry about yourself. I'm fine," Dylan said, the only indication of her pain in the subtle wince as she rose. "If we keep walking, we should hit the city limits by dawn."

I agreed. I ignored the agony in my feet and started the pace.

We didn't want to talk but the silence was too much to bear. Silence only encouraged the crying in our skulls, the rage in our hearts and the murder in our veins. I needed a distraction, anything to keep from remembering Tana lying on that slab.

"What were you going to do with the money?" I asked.

Jilly answered wistfully, "I was going to get a plane ticket somewhere warm and tropical, find a tiny apartment and just live by the beach. Everyone always seems happy at the beach. How about you?"

"I was going to go to college with my best friend, Lora."

"College? College isn't for people like us," Dylan scoffed. "That's just a waste of good money."

I liked to learn. School had always been my escape, my way of getting away from Carla and her endless tyranny. I had better grades than Lora but I didn't have the money to pay my way. I also couldn't apply for financial aid because we technically didn't have a physical address. We weren't on the lease at the shitty apartment where we lived. My mom had hooked up with some guy and talked him into letting her sublet the apartment. Lora had been on me to apply for the FAFSA but I knew it was a dead end so I was stalling. I figured I wouldn't need financial aid once I got paid from Madame Moirai.

What a colossal nightmare.

I turned to Dylan, throwing the question back at her. "Okay, what were you going to do?"

She shrugged. "I don't know. Maybe go to a restaurant and order the most expensive thing on the menu without worrying about how I was going to pay. I didn't have big plans. I just wanted to feel what it's like for everyone else for once."

It was hard not to get where she was coming from. When you've lived in extreme poverty, things that most people take for granted seem so much bigger to you. Necessities like toilet paper, tampons, food, shoes...they seem like luxuries when you're not even sure if you're going to have running water or electricity from one day to the next.

"I planned a trip to the mall," I admitted. "I wanted to walk into a store and buy something new without looking at the price tag. I wanted to buy something for my best friend, too. I thought it would be nice to be the one being generous to someone else for once. I'm tired of being the charity case."

Both girls nodded. Even if our stories were different, they were the same.

"Where are you from?" I asked, looking from Dylan to Jilly.

"Brooklyn," Dylan answered.

Jilly said, "All over but mostly Queens."

I nodded, adding my own, "The Bronx."

Jilly asked, "Did Tana say where she was from?" I shook my head. Jilly's expression dimmed. "Who's going to tell her grandmother?"

I didn't have an answer.

"Her grandmother was losing her marbles, she ain't even going to notice," Dylan said, her tone sharp. "It doesn't matter anyway."

I glared at Dylan. "It *does* matter. *Everything* fucking matters, you hear me?"

I wouldn't let Dylan be part of the collective system that told the world we didn't matter. If no one else cared about us, we had to.

"Whatever," Dylan muttered. "Pick up the fucking pace, would you? I don't want to freeze out here because you two are dragging your feet."

Dylan surged forward, leaving me and Jilly a few steps behind. Jilly struggled to keep up but she was trying. Some people didn't have endurance. Jilly was one of those people.

It was going to be a challenge to keep her from running to the cops, especially if Dylan kept snapping at her.

"I can't feel my feet anymore," Jilly murmured, mostly to me.

"Me either," I said, which was a blessing. I no longer felt the throbbing agony of my torn toenail. If we didn't end up with frostbite it would be a miracle but we didn't have a choice. We had to keep going. "At least it doesn't hurt anymore."

"I think that's a bad sign," Jilly said, fearful. "I don't want to lose my toes."

"You won't," I assured her but hell, I didn't know if I was talking out my ass or if I was right. All I knew was that we were trudging through the bitter cold with only the thin pajamas they kept us in and we were nearly frozen to the bone but at least we weren't locked in a room like prisoners. "I'd rather die of exposure than do anything Madame Moirai told me to do."

"Do you think...she was going to kill us?"

"I don't know." I thought of the makeshift morgue downstairs. Why would they have a facility set up like that? Even with a quick look at Tana, I could tell she'd been cleaned up. Aside from the bruising, she looked as if she were sleeping. Had she died in the mansion or had she died elsewhere and returned to Madame Moirai like defective merchandise?

"I don't understand why she did this to us. We followed through on our end. We signed c-c-c-ontracts." Jilly's teeth began to chatter. "We did everything she asked us to."

Dylan whipped around to stare us down. "She was never going to pay us. It was all a fucking lie. We were used. That's it. Plain and simple. We fell for her con and now we're paying for our stupidity. Best to stop asking for a reason. Shit happens and then you die."

"You're a ray of fucking sunshine," I muttered. "Maybe you could shut your trap if you're not going to say anything worth hearing."

Dylan smirked and turned back around.

If we didn't make it to a town soon, we might die of exposure before Madame Moirai could get to us first or I might push Dylan down a hill.

It could go either way.

A half-hour later, lights appeared in the distance as we crested the hill and discovered a small town. Relief made tears spring to my eyes and gave me a surge of adrenaline. We all picked up the pace to a light jog until we spotted a darkened house off the main road. We skidded to a stop, breathing hard, creating frosty plumes before our faces. "They probably have a car," I said, looking to Dylan.

Rift forgotten, Dylan nodded. "Let's go."

We quietly made our way toward the house, creeping slowly onto the property, listening for dogs who might give away our position.

But as we got closer, we could tell the house was empty. "I think it's a vacation rental or something," I said.

Jilly agreed, relieved. "No one is here during the winter. It's probably locked up for the season."

"There's probably not a car, then," I said.

"No, but we can get out of the cold before we freeze our asses off," Dylan said and I couldn't argue that point.

We made our way to the house, checked for alarms and found none. Dylan grabbed a small rock and went around to the back door. The sound of breaking glass tinkled into the night. A dog barked in the distance as we rounded the corner and found Dylan shoving her hand through the broken pane to twist the lock open. The door swung in and we hurried inside and closed the door behind us.

The house wasn't big but it was cozy. The furniture was draped in sheets to protect from dust. It was clean, which meant someone came fairly regularly to upkeep the property during the winter months.

It also meant there was probably running water and electricity. I wandered until I found the kitchen and tested my theory. I checked the tap and water flowed out. I nearly cried with relief. I turned the hot water on and waited for it to warm up. My hands were shaking as the water sluiced over my frozen hands. Feeling returned to my fingers and agony followed as pinpricks needled beneath my skin. Once I could flex my fingers well enough, I shut off the water and checked the pantry. As I'd hoped, canned goods were stacked neatly on the shelves. I grabbed a few cans of peaches and pears and rummaged around in the drawers until I found a can opener.

I returned to the girls who had found a small battery-operated lantern for a small amount of light because we didn't dare flood the house for fear of being caught.

"It's not much but I thought you might find it better than oatmeal," I said, opening each can and handing them out.

"Holy fuck, I'm starving," Dylan said, grabbing

the peaches and digging in with her fingers. She dropped whole halves into her mouth and greedily gulped down the juice. She groaned with happiness and finished the can while Jilly and I shared a can of pears.

"What else was in the kitchen?" Dylan asked, wiping her mouth.

"I don't know, I just saw the fruit and grabbed it."

Dylan jumped to her feet and went to investigate. I heard her rummaging around before she returned a few minutes later with more cans of food, including a can of Spam. "I love this shit!" she exclaimed.

She made quick work of the can and using a knife she'd grabbed, began slicing the canned meat. We each took a slice and started eating. It was practically a feast of kings given our circumstances.

Once our bellies were mostly full, we were able to take stock of our situation.

"I say we get a few hours of sleep and then try to make it to town," I said.

"I'm so tired and cold," Jilly said, nodding. "We can all sleep together for warmth."

I expected Dylan to shut down that idea but even she knew that was our best option. We couldn't afford to build a fire because the smoke might attract attention.

We might not be out in the open but the house was still an icebox.

"Fine," Dylan agreed with a yawn. "Let's find the master bedroom. It'll have the biggest bed."

I deposited our trash in the trash compactor — I didn't want to leave a mess for whoever owned the house — and followed the girls upstairs to find the master.

True to Dylan's assumption, the master bedroom had a king-sized bed covered with a thick country quilt and plenty of pillows. I looked down at my feet, seeing the blood and detoured to the bathroom to rinse off.

While Dylan and Jilly climbed into the bed without caring, I took the time to gently wash my feet, taking care to rinse my damaged toe so I didn't get an infection. I found a bandage in the medicine cabinet and wrapped my toe, hobbling back to the bed.

Dylan and Jilly were already asleep.

I climbed in beside them, burrowing down in the heavy blankets, grateful for the warmth and the shelter.

But even as I sank into an exhausted sleep,

nothing could keep the memory of Tana from my brain.

How could I possibly make it right when we had nothing but the clothes on our back and zero chance of getting anyone to believe us?

Fuck, it felt hopeless.

21

Milky morning light filtered in through the bedroom window. The light patter of rain danced on the rooftop. I rose from the bed and went to the window, careful to stay out of the direct line of sight. It'd been hard to tell at night but the house seemed the only residence for a few miles. People liked to vacation in small towns outside of the city for a weekend, which made houses like these popular rentals. That worked in our favor because it meant that it was unlikely anyone was going to pop in and catch us.

Plus, the rain was an added bonus. No one liked to take the risk of getting snowed in on vacation.

At one time someone had made this their home. A family member had probably inherited the place and decided they wanted to make a quick buck instead of making it their primary residence. A sardonic smile found my lips. The idea of having a vacation home was so foreign to me as to be laughable.

My whole life I was lucky if I had a bed to sleep in much less a house with stability and security.

That was Lora's life. I often watched her family as if staring through a window, yearning for a sliver of what they had and suffering a lead brick in my gut because I never would.

Lora had grown up with the stable parents who loved and cherished her. She had the typical upbringing, leaning toward the upper-middle class, and laughter was a common thing in their household.

Sometimes I'd felt like a dirty dog dragged in from the cold when I stayed at Lora's because as much as I craved that warmth, I never felt like I belonged.

I thought the money would make that feeling go away.

Now, I had no money, no dignity, and no future.

Madame Moirai was the fucking devil and I hated her.

My gaze found a bedside phone, a land-line, a quaint throwback to a different time and I wanted to call Lora, just to hear a friendly voice from someone I knew loved me.

But I didn't.

I wouldn't dare, not until I knew it was safe.

Moving to the closet, I opened the double doors and walked inside, swallowing the lump in my throat at the tidy contents, complimentary for the guests, such as extra towels, toiletries, and even a few robes and slippers. I wrapped the thick white robe around me and padded into the bathroom.

I started the shower and stepped inside. As much as I wanted to stand there for hours beneath the spray, I knew I couldn't. I made quick work of showering, dried off and wrapped the robe back around me. The idea of wearing that raggedy pajama set again on made my teeth grit but that's all I had. I left the room and did a slow search of the rest of the house, stopping in each of the two other rooms. I checked the closets, looking for anything that I might be able to wear instead.

A thought occurred to me. Even though the house was a rental, sometimes the owners kept personal items in storage. I found the basement door and flipped the light. Dust motes floated in the chilly air. I saw boxes lining the basement wall. I perused the boxes, glad to see black scrawl on each box, detailing what was in each.

I stopped on a box marked 'Goodwill' and pulled it down. I popped the top and found a treasure trove of used clothing. I found a few pair of worn jeans and a few college sweatshirts with a stain or two but otherwise in good condition. I took anything that I thought we could use, even finding a few worn-down sneakers.

Closing up the box, I returned it to its place, figuring that since the box was slated for Goodwill, it wasn't stealing.

Lora used to tell me I had a surprisingly strong moral compass for someone who'd been raised by a morally ambiguous she-demon. If Lora knew what I'd done, that compliment would've fallen sidewise and shattered.

I closed my eyes for a long minute, clutching the items to my chest. I would get through this. I would find a way. *First things first...*I reopened my eyes and climbed the stairs back to the floor level to find Dylan in the shower and Jilly looking for food in the kitchen.

She saw me carrying the lump of clothing and her eyes widened with surprise. "Where did you find those?"

"There's a Goodwill box in the basement. I thought we might be able to make these work. I eyeballed the sizes so I don't know if they'll fit but it's worth a try."

"You're a genius. I never would've thought to check the basement. Basements are scary," she admitted.

I smiled. "I've since learned that all the monsters are human. There's nothing down there that can hurt me."

Jilly nodded. "You're right."

I shook out the clothing and laid it out on the table for her to make the first choice. I didn't really care what I ended up with. Jilly reached for the Utica College sweatshirt, wasting no time in pulling it over her head. She grabbed a pair of jeans and pulled them on. They were a little big in the waist but they would work.

Dylan appeared, her hair wrapped in a towel, wearing a robe. She saw the clothes and smiled with surprise. "Damn girl, you're fucking resourceful." She grabbed a faded black hoodie, dropped the towel and pulled the hoodie over her bare breasts. After what we'd been through modesty was a lost cause. She scooped up the jeans and yanked them on. The denim clung to her hips but they fit. Between Dylan and Jilly, they picked out shoes, leaving me with the left-overs, a Columbia University sweatshirt with a small hole in the armpit, a pair of faded jeans with a thread-bare spot at the knees, and a pair of hiking boots.

It wasn't a shopping spree at the mall but it was better than putting those hateful pajamas back on. I wanted to burn anything and everything associated with Madame Moirai.

Jilly smiled, happy to wear something else, too. "While you were finding clothes, I found food in the fridge that isn't spoiled. Who wants some eggs?"

"The caretaker must've left some food in the house," I surmised. "At least that's what I hope."

"Yeah, it'll be a real pisser if someone randomly shows up for their family vacation and finds us camped out eating their grub," Dylan said.

It was a reminder that we couldn't stay long.

"We need to find a car," I said, worried.

Dylan grabbed the milk carton and sniffed it, saying, "Already taken care of." I looked at Dylan in question. She grinned, answering, "Someone should really give this place five stars on Yelp. They have a little commuter car tucked away in the garage. So thoughtful, don't you think?"

"Are you kidding me?" I asked, my jaw-dropping.

"Not even a little. We don't even need to hot-wire it. The keys are in the ignition."

"Someone feels pretty secure," I murmured, unable to believe this incredible stroke of luck. "I feel bad about stealing from these people, though. I mean, I know they don't know how they probably saved our lives but it seems wrong to repay them by eating all their food and stealing their car."

Dylan rolled her eyes, instantly irritated. "Jesus, Nicole, pick a fucking lane. You can't seriously be worried about that stupid shit when we're literally running for our lives. Fuck man, I can't with you sometimes." To Jilly she said, "Better not eat all the eggs or Little Miss Dudley Do-Right will have a nervous breakdown."

Dylan shoved the milk back into the fridge and stalked out of the room.

Jilly bit her lip, worried. "Why does she have to get so mad?"

I shook my head, not interested in psychoana-lyzing Dylan. She was a virtual stranger to me. Ordi-narily, I would just say, 'Fuck off' to someone like Dylan and move on but I didn't have that luxury. "She'll come around," I said. She had to. Even if Dylan hated my guts, we were tied together for the time being. I sensed Dylan's rage had nothing to do with us but everything to do with what she'd been through and that was something I understood. "I'll have some eggs if you're still offering," I said.

Jilly smiled, relieved to be of use. "I love cooking," she admitted. "Sometimes I used to dream about going to culinary school but those schools are so expensive. I knew I'd never get there."

I nodded, understanding. Dreams weren't cheap. Hope was often more than we could afford. No one ever said to kids like us, "Dream big, the skies the limit!" because it wasn't true. The reality was that no one expected most of us to rise above our station because most didn't.

"I'd love to taste your eggs," I said, smiling.

Jilly got to work, eager to do something she felt confident doing. I saw a different side of Jilly as she whipped together scrambled eggs and dry toast, presenting a small breakfast for my approval. I took an exploratory bite, surprised when it was actually delicious. "You made some magic with very little to work with. I'm impressed."

Jilly grinned, sampling her own handiwork. "I like to cook with butter but a nonstick pan will work, too. Amazing what a little salt and pepper can do, right?"

"It's really good."

"Someday I'll have to make my chili Verde for you. One of my foster parents showed me all the secrets passed down through their family. Even though they weren't great people, they were excellent cooks. People like us, we gotta pick up skills where we find them," Jilly said with a happy shrug.

For the most part, Jilly was a sweet soul. Those golden eyes told a sad story if you knew how to read. Before Madame Moirai, I would've said I was an excellent judge of character. I had a sixth sense about people. I often knew when someone was lying. A little bell went off in my head, a tiny tinkling sound that warned something wasn't adding up.

Because of that intuitive skill, I'd arrogantly thought I wasn't capable of being conned.

And then, I ended up walking headlong straight into the biggest con out there.

I should've known it was all bullshit from the start.

I never should've veered from my No. 1 rule: if it looks to good to be true, it usually is.

But here we are.

It was worse than humbling — it was crippling. I didn't know how to trust my instincts anymore. Nothing seemed to make sense in my world anymore.

Jilly seemed to sense I was struggling. She reached over to grasp my hand and squeeze it. "If it wasn't for you, I'd probably be dead," she acknowledged quietly. "I'll never forget that."

I held her gaze, secretly ashamed that my intention hadn't been to save Jilly or Dylan, only Tana and it'd only been a flip of the coin that'd put me as their unlikely champion.

I skewed my gaze away, unable to take the guilt. I forced a smile, saying, "You can make me eggs anytime you like," and returned to my plate. If I had food in my mouth, I couldn't talk and I didn't want to talk right now.

I didn't want anyone to look at me like their hero.

For all I knew, we were heading from the frying pan to the fire. I had no idea where Dylan was taking us or if it was safe.

All I knew was that for us, there was no turning back.

And if things ended up going sour, there'd be no future.

22

———

Jilly and I cleaned the kitchen, leaving no evidence of our little breakfast and then tossed our pajamas into the outside trash bin, happy to leave any shred of Madame Moirai behind. I left Jilly in charge of raiding the pantry for things we could take that wouldn't go bad and I went to find Dylan.

I found her in the garage, poking around in the bins and shelves lining the walls, seemingly more comfortable in a garage than in the house.

I leaned against the door frame. Dylan looked up, saw me, and then kept up with her search. I sighed, pushing off to walk to her. "Look, you need to cool it with the whole rage monster thing," I told her. "We need to keep Jilly feeling secure so she doesn't run off to the cops. If you keep snapping like that she's going to end up freaking out and running straight to the police, which you and I both know isn't going to end the way she thinks it will."

"Yeah, well, that's her problem. I'm not her babysitter or her therapist."

God, why did she have to be so fucking difficult? I swallowed my irritation and tried again. "I get it. None of us signed on for this shitshow but here we are and we have to make the best of it if we're going to survive. We might not like it but we're stuck together for the time being, got it? Don't make it harder than it already is."

"Why do you care? Why didn't you bail when you had the chance? You didn't have to save us." She shrugged, admitting, "I would've run without looking back."

I didn't want to answer. With a flip of a coin, I could've reacted differently. Fate had other plans. I'd never been a fan of spending too much time looking backward because nothing in my past had ever been worth looking twice at but now, more than ever, I had every reason to leave it all behind. I cast Dylan a short smile, answering, "Because I didn't."

"Playing the hero sounds all well and good until shit gets real and suddenly you're in over your head."

Her quiet statement hit a chord. I couldn't tell if

she was picking a fight with me or talking to herself. Dylan was hard to unravel and I didn't have time to play her self-destructive little games. Whatever she was struggling with, she'd have to figure out on her own. "How about you take the 'W' and stop poking at the why and how? We have to work together and that's all that matters. Like it or not, we need each other."

Dylan shot me a black look but the ire faded quickly. Either she knew I was right or she was too tired to keep fighting. She exhaled and leaned against the workbench. Her expression screwed into a mask of frustration. "I didn't mean to snap like that," she said. "I don't know...I just...I'm so fucking mad inside and I don't know what to do about it."

I understood her rage. My blood percolated with the need to lash out at someone, too. For now, I had a better handle on that powder keg but no promises that I always would. "Attacking each other isn't going to make it better," I told her. "We gotta keep control of ourselves if we're going to find a way out. Madame Moirai is going to count on us acting like scared kids. We have to outsmart her if we're going to get out of this alive."

"Look, I know you're right but it pisses me off that you're handling this better than me," Dylan said, her blunt honesty more than I was expecting. "How is that you're not twisting in on yourself like I am?"

If she knew how I wanted to curl inward and cry for a thousand years, she wouldn't think I was so chill. I shook off her backhand compliment, saying, "Trust me, I am. I'm just better at stuffing it down for the time being. At some point, the dam will break and then, hell, maybe I'll have the epic melt-down I'm due. Until then, I have to keep moving forward."

I was no motivational speaker by any stretch of the imagination but I made my point. Dylan nodded, accepting my answer. "Yeah, I guess so. I'm sorry for being a bitch. I can't say it won't happen again but I'll try to be less of a *rage monster*, okay?"

That's all I could ask for. I nodded. Dylan and I understood each other even if we weren't destined to be besties. We lost Tana. We couldn't lose Jilly, too. Through the worst of circumstances, we'd become unlikely allies. As much as Dylan would be the last person I'd choose to hang with, it felt good knowing we shared a common enemy. Switching gears, I gestured to the car. "You can drive this thing?"

"You bet your ass I can. I 've been driving since I was eleven. Manual transmission, too. My dad owned a shop. I picked up some skills when my old man was too drunk to function. Someone had to keep the shop running. That, someone, turned out to be me. Until I couldn't take his bullshit anymore and bailed."

"You liked working on cars," I surmised.

Dylan shrugged as if she didn't want to reveal too much. "I mean, yeah, it was better than sitting around the house waiting for my old man to lose his shit for no fucking reason. At least cars made some kind of sense."

I caught a picture of what it must've been like growing up in her household. Screaming, fear, pain, confusion, uncertainty...yeah, kinda like growing up with Carla until I was big enough to fight back. Fighting a man was different, though. All that testosterone gave guys an unfair advantage in the muscle department. It's no wonder Dylan was tough as nails — she had to be.

"I don't know how to drive," I said. Public transit was my mode of transportation and there was never a shortage of ways to get around the city. "But I can navigate the subway like nobody's business."

A short smile found Dylan. "It's good to have skills."

"Can't argue that."

A beat of silence found us. I wouldn't go so far as to say we were having a moment but something shifted between us. It was too early to tell but I sensed Dylan letting down her guard by an inch, which was good because I needed her to buy-in. We needed each other.

"Full tank of gas, too," Dylan said. "Like I said, five stars."

"If we weren't running for our lives, I'd leave them a glowing review," I said, hating that I was becoming a thief, too. Another crime I could heap on Madame Moirai's head. "Jilly is packing whatever we can take food-wise. I'm going to grab a few blankets and see if I can find any more clothes we might want to take with us."

"Yeah, see if you can find some socks, these sneakers are going to give me a fucking blister, I can already tell."

I gave her a mock salute and left her in the garage, which seemed to be her happy place.

I returned to Jilly in the kitchen with a thumbs up, saying, "She's good. She just needed a minute to chill out. The car has a full tank of gas, too."

"Oh! That's great," Jilly said, breaking into an excited smile, already moving on. What I was learning about Jilly was that she didn't dwell for long. Jury was out on whether that was a good thing or not. I wasn't a psychologist or anything but the

ability to flit from one disaster to another with
barely a blip of a reaction seemed like the hallmark
of a deeply disturbed person. I'd hate to find out
sweet Jilly was actually a sociopath. "And guess
what else I found while I was snooping around in
the pantry..." with great flourish, Jilly produced a
wad of cash that made my eyes bug. "Can you
believe it? This place is like the house version of a
fairy godmother."

"Seriously, what the fuck? Did you rob a bank in
a parallel universe? Where'd you get that?"

"Well, I remembered from one of my foster families that sometimes people hid money in the pantry
in false-bottomed canned goods. If you know what
you're looking for, you can spot the fake cans. The
coloring on the labels is a little off and it always looks
like a generic brand. I found one and popped the
bottom. *Viola*, travel money."

"You are fucking amazing, Jilly," I said in awe.
"How much is there?"

"About a thousand. Not enough to go to Bora
Bora but enough to keep us from starving, right?"

I nodded, happy with Jilly's find, even though I
suffered a twinge of guilt for basically robbing these
poor people blind when they'd done nothing to
deserve it. But fuck man, I'd never done anything to

deserve the shit that'd happened to me either so, that's life as Dylan would say.

Jilly wrapped the food we were taking into a big sheet, hauling it like Santa's bag of goodies and slinging it over her back. "I'll go put this in the car," she said brightly and trudged off to the garage.

I glanced around the kitchen, imagining the fun, lively conversations that'd probably happened in this space over the years and I wished I had memories worth remembering.

The solid oak dining room table looked like an heirloom, maybe something handed down from a sweet grandmother or something like that. How many home-cooked meals had this table hosted? We didn't have a dining room table. We had a card table that Carla found on the street, waiting for the trash pick up. She dragged it up to the apartment like it was some kind of prize. I sure as hell wasn't going to eat on it when it looked like a hearty bowl of potato salad might send it crashing to the floor.

I honestly couldn't remember my mom ever making me food, in the kitchen cooking or baking. Somehow I'd lived off dry cereal and the government cheese that Carla got once a month if she remembered to go stand in line at the Christian food pantry, which wasn't often.

Carla hated being told what to do and being told to show up at a specific time to get her free food was too much of a trigger most times.

I could never understand how my beloved Gran had given birth to Carla. What a disappointment she must've been.

Even at five years old I knew my gran wanted to save me but she was too old to go to battle with her wretched daughter over a granddaughter she couldn't raise.

Losing her had been the biggest blow to my young life.

What would Gran think of the deal I'd signed with Madame Moirai? I think she would've been devastated. I think that would've broken her heart.

Tears sprung to my eyes and I hurried down the basement stairs so no one saw me cry. I sniffed back the tears and pulled the light chain flooding dim light on the forgotten items. I wasn't scared of the dark and I didn't believe in ghosts. Like I told Jilly, the real monsters were flesh and blood, just like everyone else.

I found another electric lantern and flipped it on, adding to the light in the room.

Remnants of generations gone by were stacked in this basement. I could spend hours going through the boxes, wondering at the lives that'd passed through this space but I didn't have that luxury. Happy lives fascinated me. But like a moth drawn to the fluorescent light, I always got burned by the very thing I couldn't seem to ignore.

It was a catch-22. Happy people with seemingly nice lives made me yearn for what I'd never had but the flip of that coin was the accompanying bitterness.

I returned to the Goodwill box and pulled a few more items I thought we could use, including a pair of socks that Dylan wanted. I grabbed a warm beanie, a few more long-sleeved shirts and another pair of jeans, then moved onto another box marked, "Annie."

I popped the box top and peered inside.

It was a memory box of some kind. Whoever Annie was, she'd had people who cared about her childhood things. Everything in this box had been lovingly packed away, which made me wonder if Annie had died too young.

I could imagine Lora's parents doing this to her things if anything had ever happened to her. I think Carla would happily throw my things down the garbage chute without a second thought.

Ugh. No more of this pity party bullshit. I closed up the box and returned it to its spot. With a final look around the basement, I turned off the light and bounded up the stairs.

As much as I'd love to pretend that I had the right to be in this cozy house, just like all nice places, I simply didn't belong.

And it was time to go.

23

___

We left the house as clean as we could to make up for the fact that we'd robbed them blind. Thieves could have integrity, too. Dylan looked comfortable behind the wheel as we slowly pulled out of the garage. I used the auto garage door opener to close the door behind us and then I tossed the remote into the shrubbery as we left.

Jilly claimed the backseat and I took shotgun. I found a map in the glove compartment and while it wasn't Google maps, it would get us to where we needed to go.

"I think I should've paid more attention in geography class," I muttered, staring at the map and trying to make sense of it. "Okay, I think I got it. The onramp is coming up." I pointed as Dylan nodded and veered off to take the ramp.

"Hey guys, I have a wild idea," Jilly said, "why go to the city at all? We have some cash for gas money. We can go wherever we want. Maybe we could make it to California. Oh! Like Hollywood or something like that. Or maybe San Diego? I've heard that the weather is always, like, eighty degrees all year. That sounds pretty sweet. I hate the fucking snow. The East Coast with all its dreary weather can suck it for all I care."

"We don't have enough money to make it to California," I told Jilly. "And besides, no matter where we go, we'll always be looking over our shoulder. We won't be safe anywhere as long as Madame Moirai is looking for us."

"But who's to say she will? I mean, who are we? Just three kids, right? We're probably just a drop in the bucket for an operation like hers. They probably don't even care that we're gone."

I didn't believe that for a second and a shared look with Dylan told me she felt the same. "Jilly, I blew up her lair. Trust me, she'll come looking for us. We're not safe unless we—"

"Unless we what? What can we do?" Jilly cut in, folding her arms across her chest. "Like we're going to be able to do anything to Madame Moirai. It's hopeless."

I was fully aware of the optics of the situation. At first glance, we were fucking screwed and tattooed but I wasn't willing to just lie down and die. If that were the case, I would've just taken Henri's deal because, fuck it, whatever, nothing mattered.

But that wasn't me.

"If nothing else, we owe it to Tana to try," I said.

Jilly glared with a petulant scowl. "Not to be mean but I didn't know her. I'm sad and all that she died but how is that our burden?"

"How was it my burden to make sure you and Dylan got out?" I reminded Jilly coolly. When Jilly skewed her gaze away, ashamed, I said, "We got a raw deal. No one's disputing that but we can never run far enough away to escape Madame Moirai's reach. At some point, she's going to find us and when that happens...it's not going to end well for us."

"But how?" Jilly protested. "California is like a few states away. Surely she can't have that kind of pull."

"I have a feeling."

"I'm sorry but that's not a compelling argument," Jilly retorted with a huff. Changing tactics, she leaned forward with an earnest expression. "Okay,

J.H. LEIGH

yes, I get it, we're in a tough spot but we have money in our pocket, a car with a full tank of gas, clothes and food to last us for a good road trip so why don't we use it? We can change our names, get new identities, and simply disappear from Madame Moirai's radar."

"Do you know someone who can make us all new identities?" I asked. "I'm talking pass-the-government-sniff-test level of new documentation? Because I don't. It's not like in the movies where you can just snap your fingers and take on a whole new identity. This is the digital age. Our social security numbers might as well be stamped on our fucking forehead because there's no escaping the numbers assigned to us from the time we slimed out of our mother's vaginas."

"Gross," Jilly muttered, not appreciating my point. "There goes my appetite."

I ignored that. I had to stop Jilly from this dangerous train of thought or else she was going to end up dead, too. I seriously couldn't handle the trauma and I wasn't about to give up my safety because Jilly was being stupid.

Jilly turned to Dylan, looking for an ally. "What do you think? Do you think we should get the hell out of the city or stay here like a sitting duck?"

Dylan exhaled a long breath, clearly hating to agree with me on anything but said, "Nicole is right. It's reasonable to assume that whoever Madame Moirai is, she's got connections all over, which means she would've had access to private records somehow."

"What do you mean?" Jilly asked, confused.

"She knew things about me that I didn't volunteer," Dylan answered with a grim shake of her head, rubbing her forehead with her free hand. "Like personal things."

I recalled a conversation with Henri. "Same with me. My buyer knew about my mother and I never said anything about my mom being a drunk."

Jilly fell into a troubled silence, revealing, "Yeah, they knew about how many foster homes I'd been in. Down to the number. I didn't think about it at the time but that would mean they have access to confidential records somehow."

I nodded. "Exactly. And there's no way someone without connections in high places would have access to that kind of personal information. It doesn't matter if we stay here or run to Timbuktu, she'll find us. Honestly, she has to. We know too much." A chill rattled down my spine. "I know my buyer's name. They can't afford to have me out there. I'm the loose end that could ruin them. So, hell yeah, they're going to come for us. Which is why it's so important we stay together." Once Henri found out that I was loose, he might come for me, too.

Jilly fell back against the seat with a groan. "I just want this fucking nightmare to be over."

"Preaching to the choir," Dylan muttered. "If you think hanging out with you two is my idea of a good time, you're wrong."

"Hey, you're no ray of sunshine yourself," I shot back with a glower.

"Oh my God, stop fighting," Jilly said, covering her eyes with her arm. "All you do is bicker back and forth and it's driving me crazy." With a loud exhale, she dropped her arm and said, "Fine, we'll do it your way but I swear to God, if I end up getting killed because we stayed in the city, I'm haunting your stupid ass until you kick the bucket, too."

"Sounds reasonable," I said, rolling my eyes with sarcasm. I turned back around to face the road. We might all die no matter what we do or where we go. I didn't know what the right choice was but I had my gut telling me we needed to stay in the city. Dylan had people who could hide us. We would dip beneath the radar for the time being until I figured out what the hell our next step was going to be.

But how would we take down a deeply connected ring of corrupted adults? Even if they were rotten criminals, they had the veneer of wealth shielding them from consequences. In our world, we learned a long time ago that sometimes the villain won. The concept of fairness wasn't something I pinned my faith on, nor was I willing to bet my life that someone would intervene on our behalf. When enough money crossed palms, it was amazing how easy it was to turn the other cheek.

"Did you ever hear anyone mention the word, Avalon?" I asked, curious.

Dylan shook her head. Jilly chimed in with "Nope."

"What is Avalon?" Dylan asked, sparing a short look my way.

"I don't know but the masseuse said something about only the best are associated with the Avalon, like it was a club or something. Maybe a secret society?"

"Yeah, a secret society of dicks," Jilly quipped.

"Murderers," Dylan added with a thread of steel in her tone. "They all deserve to die."

I agreed, chewing on the information. "I was too keyed up to really ask too many questions, not that they would've answered. Whoever the Avalon is they have their people buttoned down pretty tight. As soon as the masseuse let it slip she high-stepped herself way back. Almost like she was scared for even mentioning it."

"Secret societies are notoriously secretive," Dylan said. "Kinda like the first rule of Fight Club, you know? No one is allowed to talk about it."

I chuckled. "Well, yeah, that makes sense. Loose lips sink clandestine illegal operations."

"Maybe we should ask around, see if anyone else has heard of this Avalon group," Jilly suggested.

"Something tells me that people who have to ask about Avalon, are clearly not with Avalon, which will put a target on our backs," I said, biting on a ragged cuticle. "It's not like we run in the same circles, you know? And I don't know any billionaires personally. Except that fucker Henri."

"Do you think that's his real name?" Dylan asked.

I nodded. "I'm positive that was his real name because he was a condescending prick when I didn't know who he was."

"Who is he?" Dylan asked.

"Fuck if I know but if he's as well known as he likes to think he is, it shouldn't be too hard to find out, right?"

"All you need is a name," Dylan said, grinning.

"And I got that," I said, returning the smile. That French fucker thought he was insulated against his crimes but that might not be the case. "So we know two bits of information that they didn't mean for us to have: a buyer's name and the name of the group in charge of this shit show."

"When you say it like that, we definitely sound like dangerous loose ends," Jilly murmured with a shudder. "If I were them, I wouldn't want us running our mouths either."

"No, definitely not," I agreed, watching as the cars whizzed past us on the freeway. "We're going to need to spend some of that cash on cheap burner phones. That bitch Olivia has all our stuff."

Which meant they also had access to anyone and everyone in our contact list. At some point, I needed to find a way to warn Lora but I didn't dare go home. Not yet. The situation was too volatile.

"Do you think Olivia was in the house when it caught fire?" Jilly asked.

"I hope so," I replied without a hint of remorse.

Dylan agreed, adding with approval. "You're a fucking savage."

Maybe. The thing was, you never truly knew what you were capable of doing until you were forced to do it to survive. Olivia was a cog in the wheel but an important one. "She's just as guilty as Madame Moirai. For fuck's sake, for all we know, she *is* Madame Moirai — and if that's the case...I hope she burned and I hope it hurt like hell before she died."

We were all thinking of Tana. I didn't need to hear confirmations from Jilly and Dylan, I could feel it.

"Do you think she died at the mansion, right below our feet?" Jilly asked, her voice choked.

"I don't know," I answered, returning my gaze to my torn up cuticle bed. I'd chewed it raw, a bad habit since I was a little kid. Lora used to slap my fingers away from my mouth when she saw me doing it. Lora was such a mother hen and I loved her fussy ways. "I hope it was quick," was all I could manage. "She suffered enough."

Silence filled the car like an oxygen-eating foam, filling the cracks and crevices, smothering us with the heavy burden of our shared grief. We might not have really known Tana but we were tied to her death in a way we would never be free.

The stark truth followed us like a tall shadow in the gathering dusk.

We were tattooed by trauma and bound by circumstance.

A trio of reluctant partners in crime.

As far as I was concerned, every single person associated with the auction could burn in a fiery pit of hell but there was a special place reserved for Madame Moirai. She financed her life on the hopes and dreams of kids who saw no other way out of their own personal hell than to take the devil's deal no matter how much it actually cost them.

I wanted to make them all pay.

And the only way to make them pay was to ruin every single one of the bastards tied to the Avalon.

They were going to regret ever roping me into their nasty little enterprise.

That was a promise.

And a vow.

————

Here's a sneak peak into the next book in the trilogy,
THE GIRLS THEY LOST

"Where are we going?" I asked, following Dylan down a darkened stairwell that pulled us deeper underground, the sound of the city above us slowly becoming muffled and distant. Urban graffiti covered the cement walls displaying colorful commentary on anything from corruption, gang wars, to incredible artwork splashed in defiant paint across the platform.

My skin puckered with goosebumps beneath my hoodie as the subterranean chill tap-danced on my bones.

Dylan, our foul-mouthed and brusque guide, didn't answer, just motioned for us to follow and to be quiet.

Secrets lurked in the shadows from past and present, whispering of an era when the subway was new and created with the promise of cutting edge technology. Time and neglect had eaten away at the former grandeur of the abandoned station, turning a once-grand dame into a wizened old lady covered in battle scars.

But this place teemed with renegade life from young to ancient. People huddled around burning barrels for heat, wrapped in ragged blankets and covered from head to toe with mismatched articles of clothing, trying to stay warm.

I'd lived in New York most of my life. I knew the stories of the abandoned subway stations but I never realized how an entire segment of society made their way down here to carve out a space of their own amongst the refuse. I was out of my element but Dylan looked right at home.

What kind of rabbit hole had we slid down?

Jilly crowded me, unnerved by the dank oppressive air in the cement tome. "It's like a graveyard for subway trains," she murmured with a mixture of awe and fear. "Who lives here?"

"Aside from sewer rats and killer clowns? No clue," I whispered out of the side of my mouth.

Dylan answered, "His name is Badger and he runs The Runaway Club. You gotta have Badger's permission to be down here or else you're gonna disappear and ain't no one gonna find your corpse."

"Sounds like a great guy," I muttered. "And you know him how?"

"Let's just say we have a history."

Jilly trailed behind Dylan, asking with worry, "Is it a good history?"

"Depends on how he remembers it," Dylan said. "I guess we'll see."

"Hold up," I tugged on Dylan's sleeve, causing Dylan to turn with annoyance. "I thought you said we'd be *safe* here?"

"We will be...if he allows us to stay...and if he doesn't hold a grudge."

Fuuuuuck. "Damn it, Dylan—"

She jerked her arm out of my grasp, her voice a harsh hush, "Look, we're screwed topside anyway so what difference does it make? We take our chances either way. I happen to think we have slightly better odds with Badger than Madame Moirai so shut up and keep walking. Not everyone down here is friendly and you're drawing too much attention."

That was some cockeyed logic but what could I say? Dylan was right. Our lives rested on the edge of a knife's blade and no matter which way we fell, it was going to cut. I could only hope this Badger was the lesser of two evils.

Good-fucking-God, why couldn't anything be easy for once? I didn't want to die in the bowels of a forgotten subway tunnel nor did I want to be chased down like a dog by Madame Moirai and her Avalon squad. I didn't have a choice but to follow Dylan and hope for a fucking miracle.

As my gran would say, "In for a penny, in for a pound."

Dylan rounded the corner and pushed open a heavy steel door that lead to a large space illuminated by an orange-tinted light, giving everything an antique look. A forgotten railway car sat among the broken and haphazard remnants of a former life, resting where it'd died, its faded bones still clinging to its identity. Bright light blazed in the car along with the distinct sound of...*classical* music and I was officially bewildered.

She sighed, explaining quickly, "Badger has eclectic tastes." But she tacked on with all seriousness, "If he asks, you prefer Tchaikovsky over Mozart and you think Beethoven is an overrated hack. And do *not* even mention Vivaldi. On second thought, don't say anything."

All I could do was nod. Nothing made sense down here.

As we got closer, I realized the railway car had been turned into a residence and it was definitely occupied.

Two teenage thugs with hard eyes and jaded souls blocked our entrance to the railcar. Dylan scowled. "Get the fuck out of my way, Roach. I need to talk to Badger."

"You've got balls of steel showing your face down here," the one on the right said without budging. "You know there's a bounty on your head?"

"It's nice to be wanted," Dylan said, not the least bit cowed. "Move before I make you regret ever leaving that group home in the Bronx."

"Still the salty bitch," Roach said with a smirk. "I'll laugh when Badger throws your ass into the pit."

I didn't like the sound of that. Jilly and I shared anxious glances as we waited for which way the wheel was going to turn on this fucked up scenario.

"What say you, boss?" he called out.

A long pause followed. Sweat beaded my hairline in spite of the chill. Dylan held her ground. If she was scared, she didn't show it but I was about to shit my pants. Jilly looked ready to faint.

A tall, lanky 20-something man with a shaved head, worn leathers, and a vivid pink mohawk appeared at the entrance, grabbing onto the poles, a sardonic but hard smile on his face. "Well, look what the cat dragged in," he drawled, using the poles to lean forward menacingly. "I never expected to see your face again. I figured you were smarter than that."

"No one's ever accused me of being smart. I was your No. 1 once, remember? I'd say that was probably the dumbest move of my life."

My eyes bugged. What did that mean? His No. 1?

Badger chuckled, considering his next move. The thick tension in the air coiled around us like a noxious fog but Dylan didn't shake or drop eye contact. The stakes were high in this game and Dylan came to win or lose big.

Which was all well and good, except she brought us along for the game with front row tickets to the sudden death championship and I didn't agree with her choice of entertainment.

"What to do with you..." Badger said, dropping down the steps as his thugs parted to make room. He stood before Dylan, towering over her. "Protocol dictates I should toss you down into the pit."

"But you won't."

Badger held Dylan's gaze as he asked softly, "And why won't I?"

Dylan stared. For a brief moment, it almost seemed as if Dylan were struggling but not with fear. She exhaled a shaky breath, saying, "Because I know who took Nova."

Everything changed in a heartbeat. I stared in confusion. Who the hell was Nova? What the hell was happening? My gaze darted from Dylan to Badger, trying to figure out why they both looked stricken.

Badger stiffened. "What the fuck are you talking about?"

Either Dylan was totally bullshitting to save our asses or there were things Dylan hadn't shared about how she ended up signing with Madame Moirai.

Important things.

My head was spinning. Jilly was just as stunned. Wisely, we kept our mouths shut, too afraid to say anything.

"Don't lie to me," Badger warned, crowding Dylan's personal space. "You better start talking real quick."

But Dylan pushed Badger out of her space with a glower. "Shut up and listen. Nova signed a deal with a woman named Madame Moirai. She wouldn't give me details but she made me promise not to tell you, saying it was all going to be worth it in the end. I was supposed to pick her up in five days when it was all done but she never showed up and her phone kept going straight to voicemail. When a week went by and she still hadn't contacted me, I knew something had gone wrong."

"What do you mean, gone wrong?"

"You know Nova would never be without her phone," Dylan said, searching his gaze. "If she wasn't answering, something bad had to have gone down. I tried to find her but it was like she disappeared off the face of the planet. I almost gave up. Then, I got a call from an unidentified number, claiming to be an emissary for this Madame Moirai. It was the only lead I had. I had to take it. I had no idea what was going to happen next."

Badger's bewilderment was almost palpable. "I don't understand. Why wouldn't she tell me?"

"There are a lot of things she never told you, Badger. You wouldn't have let her go if you knew and she was determined to make it happen," Dylan said. To my added shock, Dylan's eyes started to water as she said with a catch in her voice, "And knowing what I know now...I wish I had stopped her."

Badger paled, like someone had just kicked him in the nuts with a steel-toed boot, lodging a vicious ache in his gut. "Where's Nova?"

Dylan looked Badger straight in the eye and answered with undisguised anguish, "I'm pretty sure she's dead." Dylan gestured to me. "If it weren't for her...I'd be dead, too."

I confirmed with a small nod.

For a long minute Badger stood there, uncomprehending, unable to accept what Dylan shared but then something must've resonated with his private fears as the words resonated with truth. He dropped to a crouch, a ball of grief and anger, with a roar that I felt in my soul. Dylan dropped to the ground and held him with a ferocity that'd never seen.

Whoever this Nova was, Badger and Dylan had both loved her.

Holy fucking shit.

With sudden clarity I saw a brand new version of the woman who didn't seem to give a damn about anything or anyone but had a whole lot of fucking secrets locked behind that sharp mouth.

Tana wasn't the only one who'd never left Madame Moirai's care. The sheer scope of what we were staring down was even more overwhelming than before.

And just like that, without realizing the game was open to more players, another piece had been added to the board.

THE GIRLS THEY LOST is available now.
To purchase: THE GIRLS THEY LOST

ABOUT THE AUTHOR

J.H. Leigh is a pseudonym of USA TODAY best-selling author Alexx Andria. She enjoys writing about angsty, emotional stories with deep personal impact. You can find her on social media for more information about her books.

"Books are magic."

ALSO BY J.H. LEIGH

The Girls They Stole

The Girls They Lost

Printed in Great Britain
by Amazon